"I have a twenty-year-old son named Drew," Michael said

"And according to his mother, he wants to meet me."

A son. The words didn't make any sense at first. We had a daughter, Emma. Where had a son come from?

And then I did the math, feebly, my mind tripping back over the years, and figured it out.

"Tess?" Michael said.

I took Michael's hand, holding it hard even though I couldn't face him. My gaze was drawn to the line of framed photographs on my dresser—Michael and me, Michael and Emma, Emma alone. Each picture offered its own truth, a testament to love and laughter and family. Even if there were dozens of moments that hadn't been captured, it didn't make those happy faces a lie.

"Tomorrow, okay?" I whispered. "We can talk tomorrow."

Because no matter what had happened twenty years ago, history had taught me that there would always be a tomorrow for us.

Dear Reader,

The idea of love at first sight, especially young love at first sight, has always fascinated me. Who we are at eighteen is not necessarily who we will be at thirty or forty, and real love is a big commitment to make when you're still discovering who you are. We all know childhood sweethearts who have found happy endings, but I can't believe the road is always perfectly smooth.

Tess and Michael Butterfield are one of those couples. Not even eighteen when they meet, they fall hard and fast for each other. They're now married with a teenage daughter, and their life together is exactly what they've always dreamed about…until an unexpected phone call changes everything.

Or does it? As Michael and Tess learn together, love isn't simply a gift—it's a choice, one that has to be made over and over to keep it strong.

I hope you enjoy this story as much as I did writing it. These are characters who first spoke to me long ago, and I'm thrilled at the chance to share them with you.

Best,

Amy Garvey

PICTURES OF US
Amy Garvey

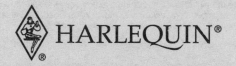

TORONTO • NEW YORK • LONDON
AMSTERDAM • PARIS • SYDNEY • HAMBURG
STOCKHOLM • ATHENS • TOKYO • MILAN • MADRID
PRAGUE • WARSAW • BUDAPEST • AUCKLAND

Recycling programs
for this product may
not exist in your area.

ISBN-13: 978-0-373-78286-4
ISBN-10:   0-373-78286-1

PICTURES OF US

Copyright © 2009 by Amy Garvey.

www.eHarlequin.com

Printed in U.S.A.

ABOUT THE AUTHOR

Amy Garvey has worked as a nanny, a video store clerk, a day camp counselor, a journalist, a Bloomingdale's salesgirl and a romance editor, among other things, but her real love has always been writing. In her opinion, fictional people are usually more fun to spend time with than real people, even though she adores her husband and three kids. When she's not writing, she's reading, and when she's not reading, she's watching far too much TV, including *Supernatural,* her latest obsession, and reruns of *Buffy the Vampire Slayer* and *Angel.* Visit Amy's Web site at www.amygarvey.com, or write to her at amy@amygarvey.com.

For April and Jess, whose story ended much too soon

CHAPTER ONE

MY WORLD CHANGED WITH ONE phone call on a Tuesday evening in May as my family and I were finishing a casual dinner of leftovers and bits and pieces from the fridge. My daughter, Emma, had dumped reheated sauce over a bowl of pasta, and my husband, Michael, had picked at the remains of a roast chicken, then washed it down with a beer. I was scraping the soggy end of a salad out of my bowl and into the garbage disposal when the phone rang and Emma bolted out of her chair to answer it. A fifteen-year-old girl's response to a ringing telephone is alarming until you get used to it, and I remembered enough about being fifteen to smile at her crestfallen face when she handed the phone to her father. Her swing of dark blond hair fell across her cheek, and she looked bored.

"Dad, it's for you."

"Who is it?" Michael asked, squinting at the newspaper he'd spread on the table and frowning.

Emma rolled her eyes. If it wasn't Jesse, the boy she was crushing on, she clearly didn't care. "Some woman. She didn't say."

He glanced up then, wrinkling his brow, and took the phone into the living room. I heard his curious "Hello?" before he was out of earshot, and a minute later I heard the heavy *thunk* of something falling to the floor.

It wasn't him, at least—I rushed in to find that he'd stumbled into the ottoman stationed in front of the huge old club chair that I intended to reupholster, knocking a stack of books onto the carpet. But his face was white, blank, his eyes as wide as I'd ever seen them, and as I watched, he sank onto the sofa wordlessly, the slim black portable phone still held to his ear.

To get the news out of him after he'd hung up took a little while. He insisted that Emma head upstairs to start her homework, a pronouncement that was met with a dramatic pout and more rolling of eyes. She usually studied at the dining-room table, with her books spread out and the wires of her brand-new iPod snaking out of her ears, while Michael and I puttered in the kitchen or sprawled in front of the TV. I never went down to the basement darkroom until after Emma was upstairs for the evening.

When she was in her room—the phone glued

to her ear, I was sure, lamenting the unfair whims of parents to her friends—I replaced the phone in its base and motioned Michael out to the patio. He followed me through the French doors off the kitchen, and I winced as one of the doors screeched shut. The hinges needed oiling, one of dozens of small household repairs we'd both put off.

The sun had just set, a faint pink-gold smear on the horizon, and our generous yard was bathed in the dusky light of a suburban New Jersey spring evening. Emma's outgrown swing set crouched at the far end, neglected. I settled in one of the Adirondack chairs facing the lawn, which Michael hadn't cut lately, pulled my bare feet onto the seat and waited for Michael to settle in the other. Instead, he paced the length of the worn gray flagstones, hands jammed in his jeans pockets.

His silence was terrifying, and I couldn't imagine what was wrong. His mother had called just that morning, and at sixty-seven she was sometimes more energetic than I was. Michael's sister, Melissa, lived in California with her family, but we'd heard from them just a week ago, and if the news concerned my family, I assumed the person on the phone would have asked for me.

There was nothing to do but wait, though. When Michael's upset, he turtles up instinctively, and trying to yank him out of the safety of that shell is impossible. With his shoulders hunched and his dark forehead creased in a frown, I recognized the look of my husband of eighteen years deep in contemplation. He could turn an idea over in his head for hours before sharing it. He'd kept me hanging about the living-room paint color for more than a week, and that had involved only a choice between two shades, Velvet Morning and November Skies.

This was more serious. I couldn't remember the last time I'd seen Michael's face so unnaturally pale. I realized I was twisting my thick gold wedding band around my finger as I waited, one of my own nervous habits, and folded my hands in my lap with effort.

When he finally spoke, his voice faltered over the words, and he didn't meet my gaze.

"That was Sophia Keating," he said, and my stomach clenched. I didn't know that name. That couldn't be good.

I could hear the first of the crickets striking up out in the grass, and the faint thump of the bass from Emma's stereo was just audible from her open window. The familiar sounds were something to focus on, because the rest of the world seemed to rush past in a dizzying blur when Michael continued, his face in profile against the last of the sun, a vague shadow.

"I...well, she's the mother of my son," he said, and drew in a lungful of evening air. His jaw was set in a hard line, as if he had to force the words out. "I...I have a twenty-year-old son named Drew, according to her. And he wants to meet me."

Son. The word didn't make any sense at first. We had a daughter, Emma. Where had a son come from? And who in sweet hell was Sophia Keating?

And then I did the math, feebly, my mind tripping back over the years, and figured it out.

"Oh." It was hardly a reply. It was barely a word. But I couldn't get anything else past my lips. Not with my heart clattering like a broken jackhammer in my chest.

"Tess?" Michael crouched beside me then, taking my hand. His dark eyes had gone even darker now, had always seen right through me. Michael knew me too well.

"I'm cold." It was possibly the most inane thing I could have said. Plus it was still warm out. But Michael didn't question me, and we went inside together. His hand in mine felt as it always had, warm and strong and slightly rough, the way men's hands usually seemed to, and I was grateful to cling to it.

We carried a bottle of red wine and two glasses up to the bedroom, heedless of the workday to come. I needed something to smooth the raw edges of my nerves, and to soften the tension strung between us, taut enough to snap.

"Talk to me, Tess," Michael said, setting down his empty wineglass and fixing me with a troubled, deep brown stare.

I wasn't sure I could. Despite the wine, which had numbed my tongue and my emotions a little too well, I was still stunned. Our bedroom was familiar in the evening shadows, the bed the same cozy, rumpled nest we'd slept in for nearly twenty years, but I couldn't shake the feeling that my life, so long sturdily set on its foundation, had suddenly been shoved to the edge of a cliff. That, possibly, it had been built there all along, held up with masking tape and toothpicks and a few ancient rubber bands. I knew exactly when this child—young man, now—would have been conceived, and what was more, I understood my part in it. Neither fact made the news any easier to bear.

Once, Michael had said to five-year-old Emma, who was pawing through our wedding photos at the time, sprawled on the wide blue field of our bed, her hair still damp from her after-dinner bath, "I knew I was going to marry Mommy the day I met her."

I hadn't corrected him, since it was probably true, even though the roots of our relationship were much more tangled than that. Even at seventeen, Michael had been confident about what he wanted, and since then what he'd wanted most was me. It was romantic, certainly, and as comfortable—and comforting—as a favorite sweater, something I could wrap around myself, grateful for its warmth, its texture, its very familiarity.

But sometimes it was overwhelming. When Michael turned the high-powered beam of that love on me, its light, its heat, could be blinding. Then again, I'd certainly never doubted it.

And I didn't really doubt it now. At least, I didn't want to. I took Michael's hand, holding it hard even though I couldn't face him. My gaze was drawn to the line of framed photographs on my dresser, Michael and me, Michael and Emma, Emma alone. Moments in time, most of them caught with my own camera, and in all of them we were smiling. I recalled the story behind each picture, too—the piece of birthday cake Michael and Emma had shared before I snapped them sitting at the kitchen table, their lips still sticky with frosting; the bright fall day Michael and I had signed the papers to close on this house, both of us terrified and elated and exhausted all at once.

Each picture offered its own truth, a testament to love and laughter and family. Even if there were dozens of other moments that hadn't been captured, it didn't make those happy faces a lie. I pulled Michael's arm around me as I settled back into the pillows, grateful for the dim light, and for the free pass I believed twenty-five years of loving Michael bought me.

"Tomorrow, okay?" I whispered, turning my head just far enough to speak over my shoulder. "We can talk tomorrow."

Because no matter what had happened twenty years ago, I needed to believe that there would be always be a tomorrow for us.

As I lay in bed that night, drifting uneasily toward sleep, I let my memory lead me back in time, to twenty-five years earlier, when Michael had appeared in my life out of nowhere and changed it forever.

I might have created him, given the right tools. His resemblance to the man I'd dreamed of, danced with, spoken to in the fantasies that occupied me while I did my barre work or ran in the mornings before school was so unnerving that, from the beginning, I found myself obsessed with touching him. A dream made flesh, or so it seemed, I wanted the reassuring proof of bone beneath skin, the rhythmic pulse of a heart that beat.

I don't have any photos of the day we met, of course. We were just seventeen when we did. The school year had ended the day before, and Lucy, Cath and I had piled into Lucy's ancient Beetle to drive to the Jersey shore. Sandy Hook was only forty-five minutes away, and the weather was perfect for it—hot and clear, with a wispy breeze. Not that bad weather would have kept us at home; the senior class had graduated the previous night, and most of them would be at the beach today, nursing hangovers and kicking off their last summer of freedom before college with sunburns, volleyball and an endless rehash of grad-night parties.

Lucy was fiddling with the radio, which was notoriously temperamental, and Cath was still half-asleep behind an enormous pair of sunglasses, her long dark hair riffling out the open window. I was curled in the backseat, my bare feet propped on the stack of beach towels, and was watching out the rear window as the crowded lanes of the parkway unwound behind us.

The summer stretched ahead, and I wasn't sure I could face it yet. Cath would spend the weeks sleeping until she couldn't take the heat in her attic bedroom any more, and then haunt the library and the record store downtown most afternoons. Lucy's job at the day camp would begin next week, and she had already informed us that she intended to paint her bedroom, too. Both Cath and I knew that she would also plow through every book on the senior reading list, and probably volunteer at the children's hospital in Mountainside, as well. Lucy, a one-girl compendium of achievements, had anticipated college applications for two years now.

And for the first time since I was twelve, I not only needed to find something to fill the months before school started again, I also had to consider applying to college. To study what, I had no idea. Nothing appealed to me. College didn't appeal to me. I wanted to spend the summer in bed, with the blinds drawn against the sun and the fan spinning in lazy circles above my head. Secretly, spending the rest of my life just that way didn't sound awful.

I looked down at my knee as Lucy pulled in

to the crowded parking lot at the beach, and examined the scar that cut through it. It was still angry, a jagged pink arrow pointing to the fact that my life had changed irrevocably in one afternoon. My parents liked to remind me that I was lucky to be able to walk, but I didn't care much about that. If I was going to be curled up in bed for weeks at a time, hypnotized by daytime TV and drinking diet soda by the gallon, two functional legs probably wouldn't be necessary.

"We're here," Lucy said, jerking on the emergency brake as the car shuddered to a halt. "Cath, wake up."

"I'm up," Cath mumbled, shoving her sunglasses on top of her head and squinting out at the sparkling water. "God, it's bright."

I climbed out of the back when Cath got out, stretching her arms over her head before lighting a Marlboro, and threw the others their towels. I was hauling my backpack over my shoulder when Lucy nudged me.

"Look at that," she whispered, cocking her head toward Billy Caruso's Jeep, parked just five spots away. "Who is *he?*"

"He" was beautiful, tall, with dark, slightly unruly hair and large dark brown eyes, his lean body delicately corded with muscle. I swallowed and felt the blood rushing to my face when he glanced up and saw me looking at him.

Westfield wasn't a small town, but there was only one high school. By the time you arrived there, you either knew everyone, or someone you knew had gone to grammar school or one of the two junior highs with the people you didn't. For Billy, a freshly graduated and enormously popular senior, to show up at the beach today accompanied by a strange boy who looked the way this one did was a social error of fantastic proportions. He was fresh meat, a new face, a walking possibility.

Lucy wasn't waiting, either. She and Billy had been on the newspaper together, and his social credentials didn't faze her even slightly. Tucking her gingery hair behind her ear and pushing her glasses up on her nose, she hefted her beach bag and marched toward him. I followed, nabbing Cath by the hem of her black T-shirt as I did.

"Congratulations on graduating, Billy," Lucy said, raising up on her tiptoes to kiss his cheek, her lips landing on the hard line of his jaw, instead. "The paper won't be the same without you."

"I'm sure you'll marshal the troops, Luce." His voice was light as he inclined his head at me and Cath. He was every inch the suave upperclassman, his baggy plaid shorts riding low on his hips, his Ray-Bans perched on top of his cropped blond hair. "Tess. Cath."

"Who's your friend?" Lucy asked, sticking her hand out to the stranger, who was watching the interchange with amusement.

"This is Michael Butterfield," Billy said, busy scanning the people down on the sand. "Just moved in next door to me."

"Hi." Michael shook Lucy's hand as he nodded all around. "Caruso said the beach was the place to be today."

"You from the city?" Cath said, eyeing Michael's H.S. 475 T-shirt.

"Yeah." He shrugged when the short answer was met with three pairs of curious eyes, his hands jammed in the pockets of a pair of faded cutoff jeans. "My dad died, and my mom wanted to join a practice out here. School ended last week."

"I'm so sorry," I said. The words sounded inconsequential in my ears, useless and small, but Michael smiled at me. A real smile, his eyes going warm and even darker. I felt my cheeks heating up again and tried not to bite my bottom lip.

"Well, I guess we'll head down," Lucy said abruptly, turning and marching for the worn wooden steps that loped over the dunes. "You guys coming?"

She'd done her duty and satisfied her curiosity at the same time, and if I suspected that she wished Michael had given her the smile he'd given me, she would never say so. Cath was, as usual, oblivious to anything that wasn't shouted, and she dawdled as we trudged across the hot sand, struggling to light another cigarette in the breeze.

But she noticed when Michael spread his towel out next to mine, and arched a plucked eyebrow in reaction. The safety pin in her left ear gleamed in the sun, and she left on her shirt and the black leather collar around her neck when she lay back on her towel. She was going to have one strange tan, not that she would care.

Michael seemed fascinated by a game of Frisbee farther down the beach, and for a minute I wondered if he'd realized where he'd chosen to sit. I pulled off my plain white T-shirt and pretended I didn't know he was there, as I smoothed oil on my legs and stomach.

It wasn't until a half hour later, when I rolled onto my stomach to change the station on the radio, that he even moved.

"Do you want some on your back?" he asked, picking up the greasy bottle of Hawaiian Tropic. He held up his other hand to shade his eyes, and I avoided his squint before I blushed again. It was so hot by then that I was probably bright red already, and I had to resist the impulse to dab sweat off my forehead and chest with the corner of my towel.

"Sure." I gave him a noncommittal shrug, and hoped I wasn't trembling as his hands worked the oil into my back in long, firm strokes. His fingers were strong, but equally gentle, and everywhere he touched felt strangely alive, vibrating with a teasing echo of his hands. I was suddenly painfully unsure what my plain bikini bottom covered and what it didn't, what the curve of my spine looked like and if my shoulder blades were anything more than bony wings.

When he finished, I propped myself on my elbows to rummage in my bag for a piece of gum. My mouth had gone dry, and I was just unwrapping a piece of Juicy Fruit when he leaned closer still. My heart was already beating hard as he waited for me to return his gaze. And when I did, he licked a drop of sweat from my upper lip without any warning.

"Hot," he said.

I blinked, and I think I nodded, riding out the potent combination of shock and arousal and curiosity. Michael Butterfield wasn't like the few boys I'd gone out with so far, kids I'd known for years, as familiar and unsurprising as my own face. From them I could imagine a cheap grope, an attempt to untie my bikini top, a casual slap on the ass. This was different.

Michael turned over and lay on his stomach, resting his head on his crossed arms so he could look at me. I knew even then that my life was going to change again, even if I couldn't predict exactly how. One thing was sure, though. The summer I'd been dreading for weeks wasn't going to be aimless or empty if Michael Butterfield had anything to do with it.

CHAPTER TWO

THE MORNING AFTER SOPHIA KEATING'S surprise phone call there was little time for Michael and me to talk. He was late for his train into the city, where he was the executive editor for a small but prestigious publisher, and Emma was eyeing the two of us over her bowl of Frosted Flakes. We were rarely all together on weekday mornings.

"Must be nice to get to sleep late whenever you want," she complained, then set her bowl in the sink and zippered her backpack. She'd twisted her hair up behind her head with a black butterfly clip, and she looked at least two years older, which was unsettling, especially on this particular morning.

"I still have to bring a note from home, though," Michael teased her. His tone was light, but the restless night had left a deep gray smudge beneath each eye. He was puttering, too, pouring a second cup of coffee, returning upstairs for a different tie, idling over the morning paper.

I refilled my mug of tea from the old china pot on the counter and said, "You're going to miss the 7:50 if you don't hurry."

"He's not going." Emma slung her backpack over one shoulder with a wry smile. "You two are going to play hooky, aren't you?"

Michael glanced at me, but I looked away, watching an enormous bumblebee hovering in the thick blue fists of wisteria outside the kitchen window. We'd taken plenty of days off while Emma was at school, spending the morning tangled in bed and later indulging in lunch out somewhere or window-shopping downtown. It was one of our rituals, a stolen day of reconnection we tried to make time for every six months or so, and we were due.

But not today. Definitely not today.

"You're going to be late, too, miss," I told Emma, shooing her out the front door with a kiss. "See you this afternoon."

Her hand lifted in a wave as she set out down the walk, and I paused at the screen door, as she ambled along the sidewalk, adjusting the volume of her iPod, her head swinging in time to the beat.

Our gorgeous girl had a brother. Biologically, at least. What else he might be to her was still up in the air, but Emma would be fascinated by the news initially and then the questions would come, rapid-fire and endless. She knew full well what year we'd been married, and she'd always been too perceptive for her own good. After all, she'd picked up on the weird vibe between Michael and me this morning, even if she hadn't interpreted its cause correctly.

Michael touched my arm, and I turned to face him. Part of me wanted the comfort of burying my head in his shoulder, but another part of me longed to crawl into bed alone for a few days and hide.

"We'll talk to her tonight," he said. His dark hair was sticking up in spikes over his forehead, and in my mind's eye I could see him standing in the kitchen, running a hand through his hair restlessly, wondering if he should join me. I knew him inside and out. That hadn't changed, either—so it was even more surprising that he didn't understand how imperative it was that we talk first.

"I'm not sure what there is to tell her yet," I argued, slipping away from him and returning to the kitchen. The pale wood floor was warm; early sunlight had flooded the window over the sink.

"I'm going to talk to him today." Michael caught my wrist before I could pick up my mug. "I arranged to call him at lunchtime. There are things I want to hear from him, too."

I let him pull me against his chest, and I breathed in the clean scent of his shirt, and the spicier smell of his skin beneath it. With his arms around me, and his heartbeat the steady, comforting rhythm of a clock beneath my cheek, the rest of the world receded for a minute, as it always had.

"I'll call you after I speak to him," he murmured into my hair, and I nodded. "And then we can decide what to tell Emma, and everyone else."

When he'd gone, gunning the old Volvo out of the driveway to make his train into Manhattan, I carried my tea onto the front porch, letting the screen door slam behind me once Walter, our aging beagle, had settled into a square of sunlight with a grunt. I had dozens of things to do, but my mind refused to focus on anything other than the fact of Drew Keating's existence.

My fingers itched to dial Lucy's number at her office, but I couldn't bring myself to do it. It was nearly impossible to get her on the phone lately, and we resorted to brief, flying e-mails more often than not, but that wasn't the reason for my hesitation. Since junior high, Lucy had been my willing ear, my shoulder to cry on, but spilling this particular story seemed like a betrayal when even Emma didn't yet know about her half brother.

As much as I would have welcomed Lucy's voice on the other end of the line, what I really wanted was reassurance. Someone to reassure me that I had nothing to worry about, that I hadn't taken Michael's love for granted, that nothing about our life together was going to change. The problem was, there was every chance that Lucy would disagree.

DANCING BALLET PROFESSIONALLY requires an incredible amount of dedication, concentration and talent. I had all three, according to my teachers, but after ten years of training, and four summers spent at the New York City Ballet's prestigious School of American Ballet, what I didn't have was luck. I'd fallen during a rehearsal, thanks to an ill-timed jump into Jared Farmer's arms, and smashed my right knee into pieces, quite literally, as I landed on the floor.

Everything I'd dreamed of, everything I'd worked for, was over in that moment, and I realized it even as I lay sprawled on the gritty studio floor. The pain was a blinding starburst, hot and relentless, like nothing I'd ever felt. My knee wouldn't move—what had once been solid seemed to be a handful of dust now, and my lower leg a useless length of bone, my foot dangling from it like an afterthought in its scuffed pointe shoe.

Now, I barely remember the round of doctors' appointments and consultations, the surgery and the recuperation. What I remember is the awful feeling of loss, and of being lost. I had nothing to focus on for the first time. For years, every free moment of my life had been occupied with dance. Studying my idols, training, practicing, living, eating and breathing ballet. It wasn't a distant spot on the horizon; it was the here and now, packing lamb's wool into my pointe shoes, washing my leotards, stretching my rebellious muscles every morning, absorbing Tchaikovsky and Prokofiev and Stravinsky until I could hear the violins humming and swelling in my sleep.

Meeting Michael was what saved me. From what, I'm not sure—depression doesn't sound melodramatic even if self-destruction does. But as intently as I turned my eyes and my heart to him, I found that I was the focus of someone else's fascination, and it felt good.

By the end of that day at the beach, Michael had asked about everything from my family and friends to what I dreamed about at night. He wanted to know if I'd ever cut my hair, which fell halfway down my back, and if I liked white peaches. He was fascinated by my knowledge of classical music—at least, the ballet-appropriate pieces—and he'd made me list everywhere my family had ever been on vacation. He wanted to know what my room looked like, if I slept on my stomach or my back and what I ate first thing in the morning.

As odd as it may seem, we didn't have anything to do but talk that day and walk up and down the shoreline, our feet splashing in the salty tide. And it was incredibly freeing. In those hours, I didn't have to think about the gaping hole in my life. Michael was filling it in with his interest in me.

It didn't escape Lucy's notice, either. "You're in love with being loved," she said two weeks later, when I'd disentangled myself from Michael long enough to join her in Cath's pool. She was hanging on to the side, kicking her feet out behind her in lazy swipes, and her wet hair was slicked back from her face.

I swam away from her, stung. Michael was flipping through a magazine on a lounge chair just a dozen feet away, his eyes shaded behind a pair of dark sunglasses and his chest pink with sun.

"That's...well, mean. And not true," I said, paddling over to the concrete lip and tossing back my own soaked hair.

"Really?" She shook her head, shrugging. She was squinting in the fierce afternoon sun, her nose wrinkled in disapproval, each freckle standing out like a polka dot. "What is it you like about him other than how he's completely obsessed with you?"

"You're out of line, Lucy." I managed to keep my voice steady as I said it, but my heart had squeezed into a tight fist. I didn't want to fight, but I wasn't going to listen to her accuse me of something she understood nothing about.

I *was* flattered by Michael's interest, and I knew it even then, but I was also pleased by it because I'd fallen so hard for him. There were plenty of things I liked about him, not that I was about to spout off a list for Lucy's benefit. He was smarter than any boy I'd ever dated, for one thing, and he was gentle and funny and kind, but there were a million little quirks that wouldn't have mattered to anyone who wasn't in love with him. The way his fingers were shaped. The way his left eyebrow was slightly crooked. The way he ate Oreos, around and around the edges until he swallowed the middle in one gulp. The fact that he was an awful swimmer but could run for miles without losing his breath. The short stories he'd written and collected in a plain spiral-bound notebook. The way he always carried a book with him wherever he went.

That he liked me was only one reason among the dozens I mused over as I lay in bed at night, and the idea that he'd given me something to do other than brood all summer didn't occur to me at all until Lucy mentioned it.

It was rude and blunt of her to say it, but there are moments now when I wonder if she was wrong.

That summer was gorgeous from the beginning, just hot enough, lush and sweet scented. The old trees that lined the streets were thick with leaves, gardens had bloomed early, and every few blocks you could smell the chemical tang of chlorine from a backyard pool. Michael had been anticipating boredom his first summer away from Manhattan, where a kid with two doctors for parents could do pretty much whatever he liked, but we kept busy in the way only teenagers seem to do, wandering the streets hand in hand, drifting lazily in friends' pools, talking for hours on my front porch, counting fireflies at dusk and listening for the tinny jingle of the ice-cream truck.

And kissing, of course. There was a lot of kissing.

I'd kissed boys before, if not extensively. I

was usually too wrapped up improving my port de bras or learning a new variation for performance, and most of the boys in my ballet classes weren't particularly interested in girls. But I had made out with Tommy Giuditta during the second installment of *Friday the 13th,* and I'd fooled around with Brendan Hastings at Billy Caruso's party over Christmas break.

Michael tasted different, felt different from other boys. I couldn't get enough of touching him. The wiry hair on his chest was fascinating. The smooth, firm muscles in his upper arms responded beneath my fingers. And his mouth was hot and faintly sweet, like nothing I'd ever tasted.

When he touched me…well, that was different, too. I was so familiar with my own body, the strength of my legs, the jutting definition of my ribs and hipbones, the painful bunions and scabbed blisters on my feet, that I was convinced it couldn't hold any surprises. But when Michael and I were kissing, tangled together in his bed or on the sofa in my deserted living room long after everyone had gone to sleep, I never failed to be awed. My body understood a whole host of things I didn't, apparently, and Michael had been the one to introduce me to them. There was heat, a slow softening that blurred every edge when Michael touched me, but there was also an electric buzz, a new, urgent energy. Need, I know now.

I was consumed with it those first weeks we were together, restless and irritable when he wasn't within arm's reach. To satisfy my parents—who had explained that although not dancing certainly wasn't my choice, I would have to spend at least some of my vacation productively—I'd found a part-time job at the cinema downtown. Michael wasn't working, since his mother felt that the loss of his father, moving out of his first and only home and preparing to leave for college were quite enough for him to deal with.

I'd been heartbroken to learn that he had graduated already—he was only a few months older than I was, but he'd started kindergarten early or something like that. I was too shattered to listen to the explanation, and anyway, I didn't care. The only thing that mattered was come September, he'd be leaving for Boston and Harvard.

One afternoon when I didn't have to work and Michael's mother had taken his sister, Jane, into the city for the day to visit friends, we were sprawled upstairs on his bed, drinking iced tea and feeding each other potato chips. We'd been talking about Michael's favorite bookstore in Greenwich Village and had drifted into a strange conversation about reading *The Scarlet Letter* for school, and then about what classes Michael would take at Harvard, where he was going to major in literature.

I could feel him pulling back, the muscles in his shoulders stiff and his eyebrows drawn together over those huge, dark eyes. He would make noises about putting off school for a year, finding a job in town and waiting for me to graduate. He'd done it before, and although I'd stopped him each time, I was learning that he had a stubborn streak as wide as the sky.

I didn't want him to go, but I didn't want him to stay, either—not with me as the cause. What if he stayed and hated me for it? What if he stayed and realized he didn't really love me, even though he'd said it a million times already, like a prayer between kisses, whispered in my ear at the movies, written on scraps of paper he left in my shorts pockets or my bag. It was then that I'd realized that being the object of love gave you power. And I was desperate not to use it the wrong way.

I pushed up on my elbows without warning, nudging the nearly empty chip bag to the floor. Michael looked up; he'd been lying beside me on the bed, his dark brown hair gleaming amber in the sun and one cheek flushed with heat.

I sat up completely and peeled off my T-shirt and bra, then swung my legs over the side of the bed to shimmy out of my shorts and panties. Michael sat up, too, eyes wide, his mouth opening as if he was about to speak.

I held out my hand as I lay back on the pillows, and he straddled me, his jeans rough against my naked thighs, his T-shirt warm and soft against my breasts. "Tess?" he said.

I didn't answer, but he let me tug off his shirt, and groaned as I ran my hands over his chest.

"This was more romantic in my head," he said as I fumbled with his zipper. "There were going to be, like, candles and stuff."

I smiled as he shrugged off his jeans. My blood was racing, but it felt good. We'd been giving ourselves to each other for weeks, fitting the smaller pieces into the bigger ones, revealing colors and shadings, creating a puzzle that was very definitely an "us" instead of the separate entities "me" and "him." I wanted to finish this now, I wanted all of it, and I didn't want to wait. "Doesn't matter," I told him, taking his face between my hands, studying the shadow his eyelashes made on his cheeks before he kissed me.

And then we didn't say anything else for a long time. But I don't know even now if I was trying to give him something to hold on to when he left, or shamelessly, wordlessly, trying to convince him to stay after all.

IN THE END, INSTEAD OF CALLING Lucy, I went inside and made another piece of toast. After slathering it with butter and grape jelly, I leaned against the counter to eat it, and marshaled myself to attend to the day's tasks. I had the Blair wedding proofs to sort and number, my own photos to develop, nearly a dozen phone calls to return either to clients or friends and a mound of laundry roughly the size of a small car.

I'd always loved working at home. Michael and I had painted, and refinished floors, and spent countless hours at flea markets and antique fairs, hunting down treasures for the dining and living rooms. It was more than our house; it was a true nest, the one place I felt completely comfortable. My house was one of my favorite places to be. But until today I'd never noticed one of the disadvantages of working there—far too much time alone with my thoughts, the usual peaceful quiet tightened into a disconcerting silence.

I made a halfhearted loop through the rooms downstairs to get myself started, picking up stray books and a sweatshirt of Emma's, tidying the stack of magazines on the coffee table, which always seemed to expand on its own, thumbing through the junk mail piled on the sideboard in the dining room and throwing all of it away. But the house was too silent, too still—even Walter was lethargic, dozing on the kitchen floor rather than barking at passersby through the screen door.

Before long, I was inventing errands to run, considering what I might need from the grocery store or the pharmacy, and I went upstairs to shower, as if I could scrub away my uneasiness. By nine, I was in the bedroom, damp hair twisted into its usual loose knot on the back of my head, rooting through a pile of clothes on the soft green chair in the corner, looking for a pair of halfway-clean jeans.

When the phone rang, I jumped at least a foot. It couldn't be Michael—he wouldn't even be in his office yet. The later morning trains were notoriously prone to delays. One hand pressed to my heart, ashamed of my foolish nerves, I picked it up.

"Hello?"

"Tess Butterfield?"

I said that it was, staring at my reflection in the mirror above the bureau, watching as my eyes widened when the husky voice on the other end continued.

"This is Sophia Keating."

CHAPTER THREE

YEARS AGO, WHEN I'D FIRST BEGUN taking pictures, I'd begun a project that I fully expected would never end. I'd started collecting old photos of my family, which I'd haphazardly stored in half-finished scrapbooks and albums or stuffed into shoe boxes up in the attic. I'd wanted a record of everyone, individually and together, and I'd pestered my grandmothers for snapshots of my mom and dad as kids, as teenagers, grinning in front of the Christmas tree, pedaling their tricycles, holding up a science trophy.

There were wedding pictures, of course, and all the photos of them with us kids over the years, but very few of them together. I changed that, much to their dismay, actually. After a while, my mother called me a paparazzo when I showed up for dinner with my camera in hand.

It was something like the growth chart so many parents etch into a doorway with pencil, mine included: Tess at two, Will at eight, Nell at thirteen. I even began to take the same pictures every year, on Thanksgiving and at the Memorial Day barbecue my parents always gave, a kind of living record, year by year, of a couple.

It wasn't just them, though. I'd done the same thing with my sister and brothers, and used the self-timer to photograph all of us together. The photos changed as we married, had children, the definition of our family expanding, fluid.

Of course, even before Michael and I were married, I'd started what I only ever called my "Pictures of Us" file. Michael, me, Michael and me together, Emma, Emma and me—you get the idea. Emma's birth had been an emergency caesarean, and although she had been born healthy and whole, I had ended up bleeding uncontrollably, so badly that the surgeon had decided on a partial hysterectomy to save my life. "Partial" meant removing my uterus, which also meant that Michael and I would never have more children, at least not naturally.

That blow had taken less time to recover from than I'd believed, and much of it was due to Emma. We were in love with our miraculous baby girl, and by the time she was three we were completely satisfied with our little family. So I had never expected that my definition of my new immediate family would need some revision.

And now Sophia Keating, the author of that revision—well, part of it, at least—was on the phone. Waiting for some response from me.

I wasn't prepared for a conversation with Sophia. Not now, half-dressed and still damp, and maybe not ever. I was teetering between gratitude and vicious jealousy—I could thank her for raising her son alone all these years, leaving Michael out of it, but I was also tempted to scream, Why? Why did he sleep with you?

The first sentiment, of course, was petty and unfeeling. The second was about as mature as my fifteen-year-old daughter on a bad day.

So instead I said simply, "Hello."

Her voice was low, a bit husky, and there was no way to guess if it was her usual timbre, or if she was as nervous as I was. "I know this is un-expected," she said, and I dropped onto the bed behind me, nodding wordlessly. "All of it, in-cluding this…conversation."

It wasn't a conversation yet. I prayed the dis-cussion would at least be a short one. My heart was banging clumsily as I said, "*Unexpected* is a good word for it."

"I know." She cleared her throat, and some-where on the other end of the line I heard a siren wailing, distant and fleeting. "I just wanted to tell you that I don't want anything from Michael. What I mean to say is, Drew would like his help, but it's nothing financial, nothing...well, it's for him to explain, really. Drew, I mean."

I couldn't help it—pity for her had already twisted into a painful knot in my throat. She was so completely ill at ease, so apologetic. Whatever had driven Drew to contact Michael was obviously not his mother's idea.

"And you need to know that I didn't tell Michael when I got pregnant because...well, when we broke off it was pretty clear he was going to make things work with you. And I cared about him—it wasn't just some fling, you know? But I didn't think... Well, I didn't want to get in the way. And I don't mean to sound like a martyr..." She trailed off, and I heard the brief note of panic in her tone. She was saying too much, getting in too deep.

Revealing things I was quite sure she hadn't intended for me to know.

"Sophia..." I paused once her name was out. What was there to say? Thank you for raising my husband's kid all by yourself? I couldn't imagine what being a single parent would have meant, and when I thought about Emma's babyhood, her full-speed-ahead toddler years, the idea of handling a child alone was enough to make my stomach lurch in despair even now.

I couldn't very well blame Sophia for sleeping with Michael, much as I wanted to. That was my fault as much as his, and not hers at all, really. Michael had been free to see other people then. And so he had.

Twenty years, a marriage, a child and a mortgage later, the idea of him in another woman's bed still made me ill. *My man,* I was tempted to screech. *Mine.*

The trouble was, all those years ago I had told "my man" I needed space. Now I couldn't envision anything more absurd. Space for what? Where was this infamous space that everyone wanted? It loomed like a gaping black hole, ready to swallow me up, regrets and all.

"It's okay," I finally said, remembering the woman on the other end of the line, who was waiting for some response from me. What a pathetic word to offer, but it was all I had at the moment. "Drew has every right to speak to Michael, and Michael is…looking forward to meeting him."

That was true, I realized. Michael was confused and upset, but there was no mistaking the flicker of curiosity in his eyes this morning, the way his gaze seemed focused somewhere distant. North, in fact, toward Boston.

"I just felt I needed to tell you that," Sophia said. "I can't really imagine what this is like for you. Not that a phone call from me necessarily makes it any easier."

Her soft, husky laugh punctuated her words, and I found myself smiling. No matter what I would have liked to believe about Sophia Keating, she was turning out to be remarkably hard to dislike.

"It does help," I offered, staring out the window, trying to picture her face, the room she was sitting in as she talked to me.

But when I hung up, I couldn't avoid the knowledge that I'd lied. Talking to Sophia hadn't helped at all. Liking her was going to make everything that much harder.

"IT'S BEAUTIFUL, isn't it?"

Struggling to keep my coffee from spilling as my sister, Nell, jerked her well-worn little Civic to a stop an hour later, I glanced across a sprawling, shaggy yard at an enormous farm-house. Its white paint was peeling, and one of the pale blue shutters on the second floor was askew, but the porch was trimmed in ginger-bread, and two brave potted ferns flanked the front door. Beautiful was stretching it, but the place did have an air of old-world, dilapidated elegance. A shingle swinging in the breeze above the picket fence read Willowdale Farm.

"It's…lovely," I said cautiously, climbing out of the car after her. It certainly didn't seem like the kind of place that catered weddings. Behind the house, a faded red barn leaned to one side beneath a pair of willow trees. Even on a bright spring morning, the farm seemed a bit sad, ashamed of its disuse and disrepair.

Nell had called before I'd left the house. Not that I'd had any idea where I was going aside from away—from the phone, from the bed Michael and I had shared for so long, from the unfinished work piled on my desk, which I knew I wouldn't be able to concentrate on. Taking a drive out Route 78 to see the place Nell swore was right for her wedding reception was the perfect distraction.

After one brief, failed engagement and count-less boyfriends, Nell was getting married. She claimed that anyone under fifty was still eligible for a traditional white gown, and she had picked one out two months ago with my mother and me in tow. She wanted the whole deal—fancy reception, bridesmaids, throwing the bouquet, everything. Of course, I would be doing double duty as maid—I refused to call myself "matron"—of honor and photographer. The wedding album would be my gift to Nell and Jack, her fiancé.

"I know it's not much now," she was saying, sweeping one arm toward the grounds, her dark blond hair swinging. She'd inherited my mother's thick sleek hair, while I'd gotten my father's unruly curls. "But they're turning it into a restaurant and catering facility, and they're only asking peanuts for anything scheduled before the first of the year."

"Okay," I said slowly, struggling to visualize the grounds cleaned up and a fresh coat of paint on the aging shingles. "But will it be done by September?"

"Partly." She was hedging, walking away to inspect the few lonely tulips blooming near the fence. A nurse for almost twenty years now, she was wearing a denim jacket over light blue scrubs, which meant she had a shift at the hospital later. She looked much younger than her forty-seven years.

Actually, it wasn't the wedding that meant so much to her. It was Jack. The prospect of sharing the rest of her life with him, after waiting for so long to find someone—that was the important thing.

"He's the one, Tess," she'd told me nine months ago over beer at the Trolley one Friday night. Even in the dim light of the bar, cigarette smoke choking the air, her eyes shone. Big and blue, they'd always been a mirror of Nell's feelings—she couldn't lie to save her life. And for too many years they'd reflected nothing but disappointment that was rapidly sharpening into bitterness.

"He's gentle and funny and kind and…" She bit her bottom lip to stifle a grin. "He's so good in bed. I can't even tell you."

"Please don't." But I laughed when I said it. My sister was happier than I'd ever seen her, and I could only hope that Jack was the paragon she made him out to be.

The thing was, he'd been close by all along. A high-school art teacher in Springfield, he adored his students and gave private drawing lessons out of the Craftsman cottage he'd restored over the past ten years. He paid his taxes, he volunteered at the juvenile center in Rahway twice a month and he liked cats *and* dogs.

"Clearly, he's perfect," my mother had teased at Thanksgiving, when Nell had chosen to introduce him to the family en masse.

"I like to think so," Jack said, not missing a beat, and everyone had laughed, including

Emma, whom I thought had developed a bit of a crush on him. What was more, he obviously adored Nell.

If he wasn't arguing about a wedding reception at Willowdale Farm, why should I?

"It'll be great," I said, reaching out as she walked past me and grabbing her hand. She looked at me, eyes hopeful and even brighter than usual in the warm sunlight. "I can imagine some gorgeous pictures on that porch and under the willows."

"I know!" She was beaming again, and she leaned in to give me an impulsive hug. She smelled like citrus and laundry soap, and her lips were cool on my cheek. "It's going to be beautiful. Shabby-chic maybe, but chic nonetheless."

I laughed and looped my arm through hers as she led me inside, eager to introduce me to the female half of the couple who'd bought the place and show me the dining room.

"Kara and Peter remind me of you and Michael," Nell confided as we waited in the drafty front hall. I was admiring the wainscoting and the vintage sconces. "They met when they were in high school, too, and they knew it was love even then. Just like you two."

There was a wistful note in her voice that I thought was more habit than anything else. As much as Nell loved Michael, part of her had been envious of us for years, of the time we'd already had together, of what she called the "lightning bolt" method of falling in love. How often had she told me, teary and heartsick after yet another breakup, that I should be grateful I'd found my life's mate before I'd even had to go looking?

"He found you," she'd said, although this was frequently uttered after a beer or two. "*Love* found you. How lucky is that?"

Very lucky, and I knew it. I knew it now, at least. Back then, I wasn't always so sure. I was still in high school, a vague lifetime ahead of me, and there were moments I felt I'd simply traded one comforting certainty for another. Ballet had been my future for as long as I could remember, part vocation, part passion, part habit. After the surgery, even after I met Michael, I would sneak up to my room before bed or on a Sunday afternoon, warming up quickly before donning pointe shoes and testing pliés and relevées. Each time, my knee had shrieked its disapproval, and my body had stalled, unaccustomed to the physical demands after months away from the barre.

Michael had offered another kind of certainty. If ballet had been my first love, Michael was my second—he wasn't so much the one as *another* one, although I'd never said that to him, and it wasn't the case now, or even after a few months together. But even if he wasn't exactly eloquent about it—and he wasn't, back then—he'd never been afraid to tell me that I was the one for him, the one and the only.

September 18, 1983

Tess,

I can't believe how much I miss you already. Feels like months have gone by since I saw you, instead of just a week and a half. I've been busy, too, getting adjusted to life here in Straus. It's a good dorm—Harvard Square is just outside—and I have a single room, which suits me. It's not huge, but then, I don't have to share it.

At the same time, since classes haven't really started in earnest yet, I don't have a lot to do but read and think about you. So I've been thinking about you a lot—what you're doing, what school is like your senior year, if your new job is all right, everything. I'm pretty happy to be here (I mean, it's Harvard. Who wouldn't be?) but in those empty moments that I'm waiting around, wishing for something to do, I'd really rather be there, with you.

I began writing a short story about this, but I'm not going to share it yet. If ever. It's still pretty rough, and in some places it keeps turning into a Penthouse letter. Not that I ever read them, you know. Really. Okay, forget I said that. Really, I'm reading poetry. All the time.

When I'm not thinking about you, that is. Have I said how much I miss you? I think I have, but it bears repeating. It's so infuriating that we met only to be forced apart three months later. I guess it could have been worse (not meeting at all), but when you find something so awesome, you want to keep it next to you. You want to be able to touch it and look at it. Now I'm making you sound like an object, which is not the point at all. (Maybe I'm not cut out to be a writer. Crap.) It's just, I love you, Tess. You're the biggest part of my life, even way up here in Cambridge.

Write soon. I love you. And also? I love you.

Michael

CHAPTER FOUR

LATER THE SAME DAY NELL AND I toured Willowdale Farm, I was trimming fresh green beans in the kitchen when Michael came home. He pushed open the screen door and leaned down to pet Walter, who greeted him with his usual drool-and-pant doggy grin.

"How's my girl?" he said, setting his briefcase down and tossing his jacket on the back of a chair.

I could sense him hovering behind me. He usually kissed the back of my neck when he found me this way, whispering kisses that made me smile and wriggle away before the meat burned or the vegetables dissolved into mush.

But we hadn't talked all day. He'd left two messages, and I'd called back at his office, only to be told he was in an art meeting. The impromptu errand with Nell had helped distract me this morning, but I'd returned to a silent house and work that refused to take my mind off the issue of Drew Keating. By three, I'd given up and settled on the sofa with a bag of chips, flipping the channels through bad made-for-TV movies and home-design shows until I was drowsy and more than a little numb.

"Just waiting to hear about your conversation with Drew." I didn't turn around, and instead thwacked the ends off a dozen more green beans a bit more violently than necessary.

Michael lifted the lid of the saucepan on the stovetop, where chicken breasts were simmering in wine and garlic. The kitchen smelled delicious. I was paying for the junk food, and probably my attitude, with a decent meal.

"We talked," he said finally, and I heard the scrape of chair legs against the floor as he sat down. "Can I talk to you now? Face-to-face?"

I set down the knife and took a deep breath before turning, and what I saw in his eyes evaporated the bitterness and resentment I'd been working into a team all afternoon. He was exhausted, and worried, and at the moment I was pretty sure he was more worried about me than about his brand-new son.

"I'm sorry." I dropped to my knees in front of him, taking his hands in mine. "I'm being awful. Tell me what happened."

He pulled me onto his lap, his thighs lean and

bony beneath my legs, and I laid my head on his shoulder, breathing in his scent and his warmth as he talked. Eyes closed, Michael's arms around me, I let the comfort of his closeness soothe the rough edges of my mood. Walter joined us, pressing his firm little body against my leg and nosing Michael's hand for petting.

"He sounds like a good kid. Kid. I guess he's more than a kid now, but it's hard to get my head around it. And he was nervous, too, which was even weirder, because he… Well, he sounds a little like me when I'm rambling."

I swallowed hard, holding Michael tighter, not daring to look into his eyes.

"And he wants to meet me. Well, us. All of us." It was Michael's turn to swallow, choking back sudden emotion. "He was kind of emphatic about that part, and he kept apologizing for whatever waves this was causing."

"But did he say why?" I asked, finally getting up to walk back to the stove. The lid on the chicken pan was rattling, and I needed to turn down the heat. "I mean, why he's getting in touch now?"

"He said there was a reason." Michael loosened his tie and then slid it free of his collar. "He'd rather tell me—us—in person, though."

I was moving the chicken breasts around in

the pan to keep them from sticking, but my mind had already jumped ahead to the moment I would look this young man in the eye. The idea was overwhelming, and a host of other thoughts accompanied it. What if Sophia joined him? How was Emma going to react? How could we be sure that Drew was in fact Michael's son?

"Tess?"

I must have frozen—I looked down to find the wooden spoon motionless and the pan lid in my other hand, suspended over the counter, dripping condensation.

"I'm sorry." I finished with the chicken and wiped my hands on a kitchen towel. "It just struck me that…well, how do we know Drew is your son, biologically?"

Michael's frown deepened, a worried slash above eyes gone still. "We don't, not officially. But I don't doubt it, Tess. And I can't ask him to prove it, at least not until I've met him."

Outside, a squirrel bounded through the yard, and Walter, parked at the screen door, barked his disapproval. I hushed him and turned back to the green beans, still piled on the cutting board.

"You're right. It's just that it's so unbelievable," I said, running water in another pot. "But too believable at the same time. Do you know what I mean?"

He was silent for a moment too long, and when he spoke, his voice was tight. "You mean it's too easy to believe that I slept with Sophia?"

I actually whirled around, for possibly the first time in my life, and water splashed over the rim of the pot, splattering my shirt. "No! No, that's not what I meant at all. It's just that this kind of thing does happen. You see it on TV and in the movies and on the news, but when it happens to you… I think you'd be the first to admit it's a little surreal."

He nodded, and then he was up and out of his chair, dabbing at my shirt with a tea towel, taking the pot from my hand and turning off the tap. His arms were encircling me, hard, his face in my hair, before I could say a word about Sophia's call to me that morning.

Then Walter woofed at someone in greeting, and the screen door opened as Emma swung through it. Her backpack hit the table with a thud. "God, get a room, huh?"

She was leaning into the fridge a moment later, grabbing a can of diet soda before slouching against the counter. Michael and I separated with a sigh, and as Emma popped open the can, he kissed her forehead. She grunted "Daddy" in a tone of outraged humiliation, but he just shook his head and laughed.

"How was school?" I asked absently, adjusting the heat beneath the beans. I glanced at the clock on the microwave. "Did you have yearbook after?"

"Nope," she said, hoisting herself up onto the counter, her sneakered feet swinging. "That's tomorrow. I was doing costumes for the play." She had inherited my mother's love of fashion, and her facility with a sewing machine.

"What are they mangling this year?" Michael stepped back as Emma aimed a light kick at him.

"They're doing *Bye Bye Birdie,* and they're not mangling it at all," she protested. "Or not much, anyway."

The hair clip she'd been wearing this morning was gone, and the thick blond mass of her hair rested on her shoulders as she leaned forward. Her cheeks were flushed, and the tentative coat of mascara she'd been applying most mornings was long gone. She looked like my little girl again, and very much like Nell, I realized.

Would Drew look like Michael?

"What's for dinner?" Emma said suddenly, interrupting my thoughts. "You two are probably hungry if you hung around here macking on each other all day."

Michael snorted, but I hid my reaction by checking on the couscous steaming in another pot.

Once upon a time, we couldn't keep our

hands off each other. Didn't all relationships begin that way, curiosity and infatuation making desire more potent, more immediate? After the first time that summer, we'd made love everywhere and anywhere we could, as often as we could, tangled together on the smelly old mattress up in my attic when everyone was asleep, reveling in the afternoon sun that streamed across Michael's bed when his mother and sister were out. Everything was still new, still a discovery, every sigh or twitch of surprise a victory and a treasure.

Of course, twenty years down the road, we felt that particular urgency less often, and sex was sometimes more comfort and communication than passion. But it was still one of the threads that held us together—I'd treated that bond too lightly all those years ago. And the incredible news of a child of Michael's wasn't the only thing rattling me. It was wondering if Michael had believed then, or believed now, that I didn't love him as completely as I knew I did.

AS I FINISHED MAKING DINNER, I thought back to those years so long ago when Michael and I were moving beyond the exhilarating newness of our relationship and into something solid, even with several states between us.

Surprising everyone, myself included, I'd applied to New York University during my senior year and been accepted. As a student whose grades had always been an afterthought compared with my form in pirouette, I'd managed to raise all my marks during the first half of my senior year—mostly because I had little to do but study, write letters to Michael and lie on my bed, moping and missing him. I'd given up the movie-theater job because the assistant manager was creepier than I could handle, especially when it was just the two of us behind the greasy concession counter on slow weeknights, and had taken a job at a bookstore downtown, instead. The owner was a wry, gentle man in his midfifties, and I was given just enough shifts to keep me busy a few afternoons a week and make some spending money.

Until Michael came home for the summer, nothing truly distracted me from the misery of being without him. When I moved into my Tenth Street dorm at NYU that September, though, it took a mere few minutes before I realized that this year distraction wasn't going to be a problem.

The dorm was a converted hotel, and the rooms on my floor were former suites, with two generous bedrooms, a bath and several enormous closets. As dorm rooms went, it wasn't the standard concrete-tiled cell I'd imagined, but I had four roommates. Living with four other girls was a shock of tempers, shower schedules, borrowed clothes and spontaneous bitch sessions about everything from boys to classes to the comparative number of calories in Famous Ray's pizza versus Sbarro's.

After a weeklong bout of what had to be estrogen shock, I loved it.

And I loved my classes, too, or at least most of them. The Psych 101 lecture at 8:00 a.m. wasn't my favorite thing, but my other classes were just challenging enough to keep me interested, and life in the Village was exhilarating. Everywhere I went there were cafés, bars, vintage shops, newsstands, record stores and people. After years of trudging only into Penn Station and then uptown to Lincoln Center for ballet lessons, I found the Village young, alive and more like a small town than I could have imagined. I hadn't stopped missing Michael, who was back at Harvard for his sophomore year, but the constant sharp pain I'd felt the year before had dulled to a low-level twinge. We wrote letters once or twice a week, although he was more consistent about getting to the mailbox than I was, and we managed to sneak in phone calls once in a while, too.

The sense of freedom was so delicious it seemed I could actually taste it with every breath of crisp autumn air. My sophomore roommates, Sydney and Marissa, were more than happy to show me around the neighborhood with fellow freshman Jane, from Connecticut, and Carter, a Southerner who constantly needed reminding to close her mouth and stop staring when we were out in the city between classes and on weekends. Manhattan wasn't unfamiliar to me, but I'd never before had the chance to make my own mark on it, staking out my favorite coffee shop, the secondhand store that sold the best faded jeans, a diner that served breakfast twenty-four hours a day and made killer scrambled eggs for just a dollar fifty.

Sharing my experiences with Michael wasn't easy, at least not in letters. He was the writer, not me, and his lazy, detailed descriptions of his Cambridge neighborhood were like something out of a travel guide. So the notion of him visiting didn't take long to be born—unlike last year, when my parents had looked at me with a combination of horror and amusement at the suggestion I take the train up to stay with

Michael one fall weekend, this year we were both free to come and go as we pleased.

"Y'all do know Thanksgiving is just around the corner, right?" Carter had drawled when I broached the subject of Michael's impending visit.

"So they can't wait," Jane argued, folding laundry she'd brought up from the dorm's basement. "It's romantic. Which is more than I can say for me at the moment." She'd had a fling with a junior philosophy student she'd met in the dining hall, which had ended in tears and avowals that Kant had ruined her attempt at a sex life.

In the end, Jane and Carter were both a bit awed that I *had* a sex life, and Marissa and Sydney agreed to let them bunk in their room when Michael arrived. The countdown began at that moment, after an excited and expensive call to Cambridge, and I spent the next week alternately pacing the confines of my room, daydreaming about what we would do while he was in the city, and feverishly trying to get ahead on my class readings so I could enjoy the weekend without guilt.

I met him at Penn Station on a Friday afternoon, hovering at the Amtrak arrival gate, dressed in my favorite jeans and a new sweater, a scarf looped around my neck that I knotted and unknotted with nervous fingers. When his face appeared on the escalator ascending from the track, blurry with sleep but searching me out with those dark, wide eyes, I nearly yelped with excitement.

The good thing is, when you don't care who happens to watch you kissing your boyfriend in greeting, you can't be embarrassed about it. I certainly wasn't. If anything, it was a little thrilling to give all those gray-suited commuters an eyeful.

That evening is still a blur. There were the introductions to my roommates, a brief walking tour of Washington Square, which was windy and crisp in the fading light and studded with gold light from the main campus buildings bordering the park, and then a noisy, crowded dinner at a local hamburger place.

I was a bit giddy—I can see that now. The excitement and anticipation on top of a grateful rush of love for my roommates, who were being incredibly generous, was heady stuff. I wanted Michael to be part of everything in my life at NYU, and even then I knew that I didn't sound quite like myself. I was babbling, laughing too loud, my cheeks hot and my pulse racing. But part of that was due to a mounting sense of panic.

Michael was friendly with the girls, and he was as affable as ever about the evening's plans, but something was wrong. Aside from those initial kisses, some connection between us had shorted out—for the first time ever, being with him felt awkward. The physical space between us seemed bigger, colder, devoid of our usual silent language of expressions and glances.

He was quieter than usual, withdrawn in a way only I would notice, despite his nodded replies to my friends. That dark head was set low, hunched into his shoulders, and his eyes were somehow too bright—they looked nearly as panicked as I felt, I realized as I stared at him across the table while we divvied up the bill for dinner and Marissa and Jane figured the tip.

The others were heading to see *An Officer and a Gentleman* over on Sixth Avenue, so Michael and I waved them off at the corner of West Fourth and turned toward the dorm. He took my hand as we walked, and I held on, grateful for its warmth in the chilly night air. Upstairs, my room was quiet and dark, the only sound a gentle shush from the filter of Jane's small fish tank, the only light its fluid blue glow.

I reached for my desk lamp, but Michael stopped me. "Don't," he said, reaching for my hand and spinning me so he could shrug off my coat. His worn denim jacket dropped to the floor next, and then we were on my bed, a fumbling, tentative meeting of mouths and hands.

But minutes later, skin to skin, hearts beating in time, everything shifted. Our bodies remembered each other without hesitation, and in those hours that seemed to stretch out endlessly till morning, we were able to find our way back to each other, somehow communicating everything we hadn't yet been able to say. Sometime long after midnight, we found the words, too: I wanted him to like my new life; he was ashamed to admit that he was slightly jealous of it; we still missed each other; college would be difficult when it meant spending so long apart.

There was more, silly things that no one but us would understand—I called him Hemingway sometimes, and he liked to hum "Tiny Dancer" in my ear to make me giggle—and then the conversation melted into kisses again. With Michael around me and above me and inside me, everything melted away—school, my friends, the world, all gone, subsumed by a rush of sensation and emotion. Michael snored as I lay there afterward, blasted, wrung dry, yet grateful that I could spend the night with him in arm's reach. It was foolish, and it certainly proved how young I was, but in those moments before I drifted off to sleep, I believed that nothing would ever truly be wrong between us that couldn't be solved by a night in bed.

WE DIDN'T SHARE THE NEWS about Drew at dinner, by tacit agreement. Emma was in one of those rare effusive moods that seemed to come too seldom in fifteen-year-old girls, chattering about the play and her friend Simon's run-in with their French teacher, and neither Michael nor I had the heart to shatter the atmosphere. She set herself up in the dining room later, books spread across the table and iPod humming in her ears, while Michael and I settled in front of the TV.

There was nothing in particular to watch, but neither of us minded. I flipped channels aimlessly, landing here or there for a few minutes, but what we were both enjoying was our physical proximity. We were curled into one end of the sofa, his arm around me, my head nestled into his shoulder, our hipbones knocking together when either of us shifted. The window over the sofa was open, and the soft night air carried the fragrance of fresh-cut grass and wisteria. For the first time that day, I was content, or nearly so.

We cleaned up the kitchen when Emma took herself off to bed, blowing kisses over the banister and reminding me she needed lunch money for tomorrow. When the dishwasher rumbled to life and Michael had shut off the lights, we went upstairs together, but we didn't go right to sleep. I slipped into bed after cracking the window to let the breeze wash through the room, and when Michael joined me, I reached for him. I was naked under the sheet, and he fit himself against me, his hard, lean length so familiar, so beloved. I let my body speak to him again that night, and he answered me, every touch tender, reassuring and full of love. *It's all right,* his body said. *I love you. I won't hurt you. We're together here, and forever.* What I couldn't hear was how he felt about having a son. The boy we'd never had. Someone he could talk baseball and beer with, another male in the small circle of our family, where Emma and I had him outnumbered. What I wouldn't know, unless I asked him, was if he was actually happy about this news.

I fell asleep holding his hand, staring at the pale, fat moon through the maple outside the window, hoping that he had heard *I love you* and *We're together* when I touched him, too.

CHAPTER FIVE

I PICKED EMMA UP AFTER SCHOOL on Friday, another watercolor of a day, soft and bright, made for picture postcards. Jesse Perry had asked her to the prom, much to Emma's relief, after weeks of phone calls and a few afterschool "dates" downtown at Starbucks. He was a junior, with the hugest brown eyes I'd ever seen, the one time I'd met him, picking up bagels downtown with Emma, and he had a distinct bad-boy air despite his honor-roll status. I wasn't happy that an older boy liked my daughter, but I didn't have any real reason to deny her the thrill of her first big dance, either. We were dress-shopping today, and I was looking forward to it.

I'd finally shared Sophia's phone call with Michael, but we still hadn't told Emma about Drew. Between the prom and the play and the approaching end of the school year, she'd been incredibly easygoing, and neither one of us could bear to share the news with her. Not yet, anyway.

"She might not be as flipped out as you think," Michael had argued over steaming mugs of tea at the kitchen table the night before. "We weren't married then. Kids are a lot more sophisticated these days, for better or worse."

"Kids are a lot more sophisticated about cell phones and fashion and movie sex," I said wearily. "Real-life stuff is a little different. There's a lot of child left in her, Michael. She still won't let me give away her Barbies."

She had to know, of course. And we were going to tell her, this weekend probably, when we were all at home together, with time to talk. Michael had spoken to Drew again yesterday, and we'd agreed that we would drive up to Cambridge over the Memorial Day weekend to meet him. I hadn't really faced the fact that the trip was only two weeks away—denial was so easy to slip into, a comfortable old coat I donned every day now. If I pretended that we had all the time in the world to tell Emma, I could almost make myself believe it.

I'd pulled the Jeep up to the curb in front of the school, under an ancient elm that dappled the hood with shadows in the afternoon sunlight. I had the radio on louder than usual, a Springsteen song from my own high-school years, and I felt pretty good—I'd forced myself through yoga that morning, which I'd let slip all week, and I'd finished sorting photos for another chapter in my book. The laundry had piled up again, but I had decided not to care about that. Dirty clothes were the least of my problems this week, and the afternoon was too lovely to spoil with regret—of any kind.

Emma banged through the front doors of the school with a gang of other girls, a rainbow of pastel shirts and short skirts, faded denim and backpacks adorned with key chains and cell phones. I didn't wave—I knew better. But she smiled when she climbed into the car beside me and slammed the door shut. "Let's shop," she said.

I shifted the Jeep into gear. "That's the plan."

We decided to start at Lord & Taylor, which would have the widest selection, if not the best prices. Guilt lay at the bottom of that decision, and I wasn't going to try to deny it. Finding out that she had a half brother, that her dad had actually slept with someone other than her mom once upon a time, when she'd long believed in the fairy-tale, childhood-sweethearts version of our life together, was going to be horror enough that it was comforting to pretend I could buy her understanding with an expensive dress.

We clashed from the start, which shocked me.

Emma had her moods, like any red-blooded American fifteen-year-old, but we got along ninety percent of the time. She still liked good-night kisses and the occasional lazy Saturday-morning cuddle, for God's sake, so I didn't expect a battle over something that was meant to be a pleasure. While I was fingering lovely, sleek little dresses that she proclaimed "boring" and "way momlike," everything she chose was either too short or was so obnoxiously glittery most Atlantic City showgirls would have protested.

"It's a prom, not a cabaret act," I snapped, hanging up the latest offending dress as the first sharp fingers of a headache gripped the back of my skull.

"God, Mom." Emma rolled her eyes and walked toward another rack, declaring over her shoulder, "It's, like, the twenty-first century, you know?"

"I know full well what century it is," I hissed, hating the sound of my voice. Where had it come from? My mother had never raised her voice, never lost her cool—she had an amazing ability to disengage whenever any of us were acting up. She'd simply pull back, eye us coolly and wait until we realized that she wasn't going to put up with whatever it was we had done or said.

I took a deep breath and sank into one of the

chairs set against a mirrored column. I could be calm. I would be calm. I had to be, about the dress and everything else. We weren't going to get through the next couple of weeks otherwise.

"Maybe Nana could make me something," Emma said suddenly, chewing her bottom lip. Her backpack was slung carelessly over one shoulder and her arms were folded across her chest. It sounded like a truce, even if it looked like defiance. My mother wouldn't make her anything too daring, but Emma would convince her grandmother to design something with a hint of sex to it, even if it was subtle.

"Nana's pretty busy right now, Em," I said carefully. "You could ask her this weekend, but I can't guarantee she'll be able to make you a dress before the dance."

"I bet she'll do it."

"Well, we'll find out, I guess." I stood up and started for the door, Emma following beside me without a word. I didn't understand her abrupt about-face—at least, not until we got into the car and I was steering out of the parking lot.

"Jesse invited me to a party," Emma said, fiddling with a tube of lip gloss she'd scrounged out of her bag.

"After the prom, you mean?" I needed to

make a left onto North Avenue, which was nearly impossible at that time of day.

"No, Memorial Day."

Damn it. Those same fingers pinched into my skull. The battle hadn't been won; the venue had simply changed.

"Emma, I don't know…"

"It's at his parents' house," she said quickly. She'd rolled down her window, and a rush of air blew her hair back as I saw my opportunity and pulled onto the road.

"I haven't met his parents, Emma, and I don't think—"

She cut me off. "They're really nice, Mom. And Grace is going, too. Her mom said yes."

There it was, the resentful emphasis on the word *her.* Other parents understood, that tone said. Other parents were *cool.*

Of course, other parents were probably not driving two hundred miles that weekend to meet a newly discovered illegitimate son.

"Well, Grace can tell you all about it," I said in the most even tone I could manage. "But that weekend is a problem."

"I knew you'd say no. I knew it! I didn't even have to tell you the party's at their shore house. I told Grace I wouldn't get that far." Arms folded across her chest again, she was seething, her jaw tight with fury and her eyes brimming with tears.

I couldn't even pretend sympathy at the moment. "At their *shore* house? The party is at their shore house, and you thought you had a chance to go?"

The tears spilled, bright wet tracks down her cheeks. "Grace is going!"

"Well, I'd love to know if Grace's mother was told exactly where this party is." I turned off North onto Dudley with a jerk of the steering wheel.

Silence.

I kept my mouth shut, too. It was the smart move at the moment, with my headache ramping up again, more vicious than before, and my heart still hammering in outrage. A party at the beach, fifty or more miles away, with a boy I'd barely met? She was dreaming. Even if Jesse's parents were there, which was iffy, it didn't mean the kids would be supervised down at the beach. And God knows I had a good idea what teenagers could get up to when they were determined.

She was too young still, a child beneath the tentative makeup and the clothes and the newly adopted attitude. She had no idea about boys, older boys, and certainly not about sex… She didn't, did she? Oh God—my headache, and everything else, was going from bad to worse.

"Why exactly is Memorial Day a problem?" Emma said, startling me out of my thoughts.

I swung the Jeep onto Clark, my teeth clenched. What was I supposed to tell her?

"Mom?" Resentful, demanding.

"We'll discuss it when your father comes home," I said, turning down our street and into the driveway.

She huffed "Whatever" and slammed out of the car, leaving me leaning against the steering wheel, my heart still hammering, the afternoon sun hot on the knuckles that gripped the wheel. Through the screen door she'd left open, I heard a door bang shut, then Walter's confused whine.

What the hell had happened? I'd imagined a fun afternoon, giggling over dresses, maybe shopping for shoes, too, or stopping off at Starbucks for lattes when we were done. And what had happened to the sweet, happy kid who'd been humming around the house all week, doing her homework without prodding, even picking up her dirty clothes and unloading the dishwasher?

I got out of the car and went inside, stooping to scratch Walter's soft head. Tossing my bag on the kitchen table, I dropped onto a chair with a sigh. It wasn't too hard to figure out, once I thought about it. She'd been imagining what might have been, daydreaming each conversation between her and Jesse, each accidentally-on-purpose touch, probably each kiss. She'd been contentedly building a whole relationship based on what-ifs, and it had played out beautifully until I'd dragged her back to reality.

I couldn't blame her for the tantrum, not really. Laying my head down on my folded arms, suddenly and completely exhausted, I closed my eyes, only faintly aware of the pounding beat of Emma's stereo through the ceiling. I'd daydreamed a whole relationship once myself.

HIS NAME WAS CYRUS CAMPBELL. I met him in my art history lecture sophomore year when he slid into the battered auditorium seat next to mine just moments before class was supposed to start.

"Made it," he whispered, winking at me. Muddy hazel eyes peeked out from beneath a fringe of hair, tarnished gold, thick and uncombed.

I think I blinked in response. He smelled like coffee and cigarettes, and faintly of turpentine, and his army jacket was still damp from the morning rain. He seemed enormous in those cramped seats, too big, too noisy, boots clunking against the worn linoleum, unzipping his backpack with abandon, sighing as he settled in to wait for the lecture to begin.

Professor D'Angelo gave us the course overview that day, the syllabus and the standard admonitions about attendance and exams, but when I left, I couldn't remember a word of it. Cyrus was as fascinating as he was irritating.

A shaggy, carefree lion. That was what he reminded me of, with all that long, dirty-blond hair and those strange eyes, the casual grace of his body, slouched in a chair or loping across the park, unconcerned with his surroundings.

And he was everywhere that semester, or seemed to be. In the dining hall, at the newsstand where I bought the occasional magazine and Mounds bars when I was stressing about class work. At the diner over on Astor Place, where Carter and I liked to have cheap omelets and coffee late on Saturday mornings, and in the library when I needed to concentrate on the history of the Renaissance. Big and blond, that slow, steady smile aimed at me like an arrow.

Even at such a huge university, the grapevine was pretty efficient if you knew how to work it. Within a couple of days I'd discovered he was a math major who liked to paint, he was from Denver and his roommate was premed and incredibly tense about noise.

"Doesn't own a stereo and wears earplugs in the dorm," Jane told me with a raised eyebrow. "Sounds like a barrel of laughs."

"Cyrus must love him," Carter put in with a giggle. She was sprawled on her bed with the notes for her poetry paper scattered around her like the aftermath of a cyclone. "Sounds like the Odd Couple Goes to College."

Cyrus was definitely the opposite of tense. Nothing bothered him, not impending exams or lost lecture notes, not the gray, interminable rain that autumn, not my regretful no when he asked me out.

"Okay," he said, strolling along next to me as we walked out of the lecture auditorium after psychology one day. "I'll take that as a 'not now'. And if you change your mind, just say so."

He was nothing like Michael, not physically or temperamentally, and not what I would have considered my type, either. But I couldn't deny that I was attracted to him—everything seemed easy and more fun when he was around. During psych lectures he doodled caricatures to me in the margins of my notebook. He smuggled extra Jell-O onto his dinner tray for me in the dining hall. He was always smiling, and usually laughing.

Michael had never been so easygoing. He wasn't tense, necessarily, but *intense* wasn't the wrong word. He came off as laidback to the rest of the world, but inside he was usually brooding about something, examining thoughts and reactions in his head, figuring out what any given situation meant. Everything *mattered* to Michael.

And not much ever mattered to Cyrus. Not my refusal of a date, not the C- he received on his psych midterm, not the news that a bar underage students had counted on for more than twenty years was closing.

"Somebody will find another place that'll serve us," he said with a shrug. We were in the laundry room in the dorm's damp basement, waiting for the spin cycle to end so we could load the dryers and head back upstairs to the lounge.

Lopsided optimism, that was what it was. Michael wasn't pessimistic, but he was an idealist, a romantic, which meant that life sometimes didn't live up to his expectations. As far as I could tell, Cyrus didn't have any.

"We're not doing anything," I told Jane when she remarked on the fact that Cyrus and I had eaten lunch together at Eddie's, a little pub on West Third. "We're just friends."

Lips pursed in disapproval, she'd raised her eyebrows, but she didn't say more.

Across the room at her desk, Carter sighed. "Leave her alone, Jane. She's a big girl. If she wants to break that sweet Michael's heart, that's her call."

Of course I didn't want that. I threw my tattered stuffed pig at her, but she ducked and stuck her tongue out at me.

I didn't want to stop seeing Cyrus, either, though. It wasn't cheating; we weren't kissing or even holding hands. But when he walked me back to the dorm after class, I couldn't stop myself from imagining what it would be like if his arm were looped around me. What his mouth would taste like, whether that shaggy gold hair would brush my cheek if he kissed me.

The physical attraction wasn't the only temptation. I had the feeling that Cyrus wouldn't mind if I spent a weekend away from him, that he wouldn't write me letters several pages long each week, that he wouldn't be particularly interested in what I was reading or what movies I'd been to.

And I knew, deep down, that anything I felt for Cyrus would be light, nothing more than a gentle breeze washing through my life briefly. With Cyrus, I would never feel that sometimes frightening sense of obliteration, of losing myself in what I felt for him and how much he mattered to me—of not being able to love him well enough, the way I sometimes did with Michael.

EMMA CONTINUED RADIO silence all afternoon. The door to her room was firmly shut, and behind it the sound of her stereo was an angry drumbeat. She never emerged, not that I asked her to, not even for a soda or a snack, not even to go to the bathroom, as far as I could tell. I left her alone, letting my own thoughts stew.

Michael got home shortly after six. He took one look at my face as I glanced up from the fridge, where I'd been contemplating dinner, and dropped his briefcase on the table to put his arms around me.

"What happened, babe? No good dresses?"

I leaned into him, breathing in the clean, warm scent of his skin. "Nope. No good anything, not this afternoon."

He stroked the back of my head, and I pushed gently against his hand, grateful for his touch. "Tell me," he said.

"Every dress she wanted looked like something you'd find on Eleventh Avenue at 2:00 a.m., and she also wants to go to some party at Jesse's house." I paused for effect. "At the shore. Memorial Day weekend."

His eyes widened in disbelief, but just as he

opened his mouth to protest, we heard Emma pounding down the stairs.

She appeared in the doorway to the kitchen a moment later, cheeks flushed, eyes still faintly swollen. Her hair looked as if she'd used an eggbeater to comb it.

Without any buildup, she said, "What's going on Memorial Day weekend?" Sullen and resentful, her voice a jagged knife in the silence.

I released a breath and untangled myself from Michael's arms to sit down. This was not the way I'd imagined conducting this particular conversation, but there was no point putting it off any longer. I glanced at Michael, who was still recovering from the shock of Emma's request, and he gave me a grim smile.

"Sit down, Emma." I motioned to the chair opposite me.

She crossed her arms in front of her, hipshot and more defiant than ever. "I'm fine."

Walter was circling the kitchen, panting at Michael's feet and then crossing to Emma, who ignored him. I tapped my thigh and he settled next to me, quivering with need and alert to the current of tension rippling through the room.

"Sit down, Emma."

Michael rarely reprimanded her, but what I called his Father-Knows-Best voice never failed to do the trick. She sidled past me and scraped a chair away from the table, dropping into it with a definite flounce.

"What?" He waited silently until she raised her eyes before answering.

"We need to have a discussion, but if you're not prepared to be polite, it will have to wait." He slid another chair around to the side of the table, between us, refusing to take a side. I longed to hold his hand beneath the table, but I controlled myself. Emma was near tears again.

"I'm sorry." Emma's voice was little more than a whisper. "We can talk."

"Aside from the fact that going to a party at the shore, fifty miles away or more, is out of the question," he said, holding up a hand when she opened her mouth to argue the point, "we have something important to do on Memorial Day weekend. Important to me, at least."

"We never do anything but cook out at Nana's that weekend," Emma grumbled. She was examining a fingernail with exaggerated interest.

Shit. I had forgotten about the barbecue my parents usually hosted, although I wasn't sure how. We'd gathered there every year since before Emma was born, with Nell and my brothers attending whenever they were around. The barbecue was a given, a comfortable tradition that revolved around homey food and relaxation in my parents' backyard, whatever ball game was on and the light, pleasant buzz of a couple of beers consumed in the first of the summer heat. Hell, it was one of the times I took my traditional photographs of Mom and Dad and the rest of the family.

Michael sighed, his brow knotted in frustration. I nodded permission, and he said, "This year we're skipping it."

"So what's the big drama?" Emma asked. She'd pulled her knees up to her chest, her heels balanced on the edge of her seat, and now she wrapped her arms around her legs. In the gold shimmer of the evening sun through the window above the sink, her eyes burned with questions and newborn anxiety.

Michael cleared his throat, and when the silence stretched out too long, I gave up and reached out to hold his hand. His fingers tightened around mine, and I sat up straighter.

"Do you remember that someone called the other night? A woman?" I began. God, it was hard. Speaking the words made this whole situation real, not just some disturbing dream Michael and I had shared.

Emma nodded, but she was frowning already. Beside me, Michael shifted. I swore I could feel his pulse speed up, his muscles going taut in preparation.

"She was a woman Daddy used to know. A long time ago, before we were married," I hurried to add. "Daddy and I… Well, that's not important, really. But what is important is that this woman…"

The tears were unexpected, a hot rush in my throat, and I swallowed to hold them back.

"We had a child together, Em," Michael finished. His voice was rough, but it was strong. I squeezed his hand as he went on. "She never told me about it. What I mean is, when we separated, I didn't know she was pregnant. I guess she had her own reasons not to tell me. But now—"

"You have a…a kid?" Emma broke in, her soft mouth trembling. "Some other kid, with some random woman?"

"She's not some random woman," Michael said, and I flinched at the sharp edge of his tone. Or was it the words he'd used? "Sophia and I had a relationship, but it didn't work out in the end. I loved your mother—"

"Then why were you with someone else?" Emma wasn't crying, but she was panicking. Her voice had gone up at least an octave, and she was hugging her legs so tightly to her chest her fingers had left marks on her bare calves.

"It's complicated." I got up and walked around the table, and she let me draw her into my arms. She was trembling, running hot with adrenaline and emotion, and I stroked her hair the same way I had when she was a toddler curled on my lap after a fall. "What's important right now is that this…boy would like to meet Daddy. All of us, actually."

She shook her head as if she could make the knowledge disappear, but then she asked, "What's his name?"

"Drew," Michael told her. I met his dark, tired gaze. "He's twenty, and he lives in Boston. That's where we're going Memorial Day weekend. To meet him. I owe him that, Emma."

"You owe…?" She pushed away from me suddenly, and then out of the chair, the tears finally coming. She was gulping, shuddering, caught somewhere undefined between the child she'd been and the young woman she was becoming. I reached for her, but she flinched and ran for the door, shouting over her shoulder, "Well, I don't! God, I don't… And I'm not going!"

CHAPTER SIX

"WHAT'S WRONG WITH EMMA TODAY?" my mother asked on Sunday. She was icing an angel food cake, and she glanced up from the counter, spatula in hand, to look at me. I was shredding lettuce for a salad—she'd decided on a casual lunch to celebrate Dad's birthday, since he wasn't big on crowds or what he called "making a fuss," and next year he would be seventy-five. Mom was already planning to make a fuss then, whether he liked it or not.

"She's fifteen," I said of Emma, keeping my tone light. "Something's always wrong at that age, remember?"

Emma had barely left her room on Saturday. I hadn't even heard her stereo, which meant she'd probably been huddled in bed with her iPod. She'd emerged at one, taken two cans of diet soda and a bag of chips up to her room, feet heavy on the stairs, and at dinnertime she'd come to the table only after Michael had called her for the third time, and then had sat hunched over her plate of pizza, stony and silent. She hadn't showered, so her hair was lank, and she was wearing an old blue sweatshirt of Michael's.

I hadn't pressed the issue of us driving up to Cambridge, and neither had Michael, although we'd made it clear that we were willing to talk about Drew, and what she was feeling, whenever she was ready. When she asked when we could discuss Jesse's party, instead, her eyes direct and her voice flat, I'd dropped my napkin on my plate and walked out of the room.

I had been that self-centered at her age, and I knew it. My mother would agree, and there was no question that she would say so to anyone within hearing distance if I brought it up. That knowledge didn't make Emma's sullen resentment any easier to stomach, and Michael was sick about it.

"What if she hates me?" he'd said, sitting beside me on the front porch swing that evening when she'd gone back upstairs. "What if this destroys our relationship? Drew may have some of my DNA, but Emma is my *daughter.* Emma and you are everything to me, Tess. Everything. How am I supposed to feel about all this? There's no choice to be made, if that's what he's asking." He'd squeezed my hand as he said it, and when I glanced at him in the velvety dusk, his eyes were bright with tears.

Curling into him, tucking my head into his shoulder, I'd simply pushed off the gritty porch floor with one toe, sending the swing into motion. No matter how deeply he felt something, Michael was still a guy, and he rarely cried. One of the last times I'd seen tears in his eyes had been the day Emma was born, in fact, when the nurse had handed her over, squalling and pink and furious. That night I was afraid that if he started, he wouldn't be able to stop—and that I wouldn't be able to comfort him. I was hardly able to comfort myself, and certainly not my daughter.

We'd agreed not to bring up the subject today at my parents', either. It was Dad's day, and Michael's mom had been invited—she and my parents had become friends long ago, which was an unexpected pleasure. More than polite in-laws, they enjoyed spending time together, and in the past couple of years my mother and Maureen had made a tradition of spending a weekend or two together either in Manhattan or at the beach, shopping and eating out and, I suspected, discussing their children with the fond, if critical, interest of mothers.

My brother Matt had arrived today with his

wife, Robin, and their two little boys, since they would be at the shore over Memorial Day. Will, the baby at thirty-nine, was in Virginia, and Nell had to work, although Jack had come, hoisting a six-pack of my father's favorite beer and a new book about some famous physicist for him to read. It added up to too many people, too many potential questions and far too many uncomfortable possibilities.

My mother, of course, wasn't going to accept my offhand answer about her grand-daughter at face value, though. Since we'd practically had to drag Emma out of the house, I wasn't exactly surprised that Mom had picked up on her mood. She'd taken a book onto the back porch nearly the minute we'd arrived an hour ago, and hadn't reappeared since.

"She seems upset, Tess, not just moody," Mom said, licking strawberry icing off the spatula. "Anything going on?"

"It's okay, Mom." I finished the salad with a generous handful of sliced green pepper. Opening the fridge to put the cucumber away, I spotted a few Polaroids of Mom's latest dresses stuck to the freezer door with magnets, and inspiration struck. "We had an argument about what kind of dress she wanted for this dance she's been invited to, and I think she's going to ask you if you'll make her something."

My mother licked another smear of strawberry frosting off her index finger, then smiled. She'd retired years ago after working as a children's-wear designer, but she hadn't stopped designing clothes or sewing.

"I can probably manage something. Especially something that won't remind one of Britney Spears on a particularly trashy day." She set the glass cover over the cake plate and opened the door to the back porch. "I'll go talk to her now."

Oh, good. I swallowed my discomfort as I leaned into the fridge to grab the platter of Chinese chicken salad, but just then Eli and Owen slid into the kitchen in their socks.

"It is so mine! Give it back," Owen shouted. His round face was red with fury.

"It's *mine,* you booger," Eli taunted him, scrambling past me, holding a battle-scarred Spider-Man action figure above his head.

Mom grabbed it up neatly and tucked it in her shirt, between her breasts, just as Robin and Matt appeared in the doorway, humiliation and frustration warring on their faces.

"Eli." Matt was glowering, and Robin's lips were pressed into a tight line as she marched six-year-old Owen out of the kitchen.

"It's all right," Mom said, smiling innocently at nine-year-old Eli, who was staring in shock at his grandmother's neckline. "I have the toy in question, and I'm sure that after a little discussion the boys will work out a way to share it. If not, there's always some weeding that needs to be done."

Matt muffled a laugh as Eli's eyes widened, and a moment later he followed his father into the living room without an argument.

"Boys are so easy to manipulate, aren't they?" my mother said with a grin, extracting Spider-Man from her blouse and squinting at him. "I was always a Batman fan myself."

I snorted, and just then Dad and Michael walked into the kitchen, sniffing the air like a pair of puppies. "When are we eating? I'm starved," Dad said, putting his arm around me and squeezing. "How's my gorgeous daughter?"

"Fine, Daddy." I stretched up to kiss his cheek. It was cool and papery now, which was always surprising, but it smelled like him— clean, with a breath of sandalwood. I had an urge to throw my arms around him, climb into his lap, let him sort out everything, or at least pretend to while he whispered soothing nothings against my ear.

If I closed my eyes, I'd be seven again, or

twelve, or sixteen, standing in the kitchen where I'd grown up, with all its familiar scents—the hydrangea through the window, my mother's Chanel No 5, the sharp odor of the cat litter on the basement-stairs landing.

Nothing had changed, and everything had. I wasn't that little girl anymore, but I remembered her, the moments she'd wanted nothing more than the comfort of her parents' reassurance, and God, what I wouldn't give for that now. The trouble was, there was a lot more at stake than passing a test or being chosen as a soloist in the spring ballet recital. It was my marriage, my child, my life. And not for nothing, my parents' love for Michael.

They adored him. Oh, at first they'd been a little wary—he was new in town, he was heading off to college and from the beginning we'd been attached at the hip like a couple of long-lost twins, scarily obsessed with each other, all hands and eyes. We'd been so young when we'd met, which was easy enough to admit now that we weren't, that it was sometimes curious they hadn't protested our constant togetherness more vigorously, although my mother had had her objections that first year.

Of course, Michael had been a good kid, and he'd become a wonderful man. I gave them credit for recognizing everything I loved about him, and for loving him themselves like another son. If that changed because of something that was as much my fault as his…

I couldn't even follow through with the thought, and when I realized my cheeks had gone hot and my throat was choked with tears, I had to wriggle out from beneath my father's arm, pretending a sudden need to find a soda in the fridge.

"Let's eat, huh?" I said as brightly as I could manage, still facing the cool inside the refrigerator. "Michael, you want to go grab Emma?"

The silence hummed with tension, but finally Michael said, "Mom, should I round up the boys, too? I think they ran outside."

I took a deep breath and found my mother's dark blue eyes narrowed at me in concern. Dad had his finger in the icing bowl, oblivious, so I simply smiled and carried the platter of chicken salad into the dining room, where Robin had set the table.

The windows were open, and a warm breeze blew the old muslin curtains away from the sills. Minerva, Mom's oldest cat, was curled on one of them, her orange tail flicking in and out in a lazy rhythm.

"There are days I prefer cats over kids,"

Robin said from behind me. "And I don't really like cats."

I laughed, although the sound was a little rusty in my throat. "They're good boys. They're just…boys. Of a certain age."

She made room for the platter I was still holding by moving a pair of tarnished candlesticks to the sideboard. As always, she was crisp and pressed today, in clean khakis and a thin black sweater, black loafers on her feet, her auburn hair straight and glossy, tucked behind her ears. I was never sure exactly what it was she did for a living, except that she worked in administration at Rutgers and it seemed to suit her—or at least, my impression of her. Robin liked to organize, to file and label and give things a place. Parenthood had been tough for her in the beginning. When she'd had Eli, she'd spent as much time labeling Baggies of breast milk as she had cuddling him, and she was obviously much more comfortable with the former.

Still, I liked her. She was friendly, if not exactly easygoing, and the few times I'd been alone with her—Christmas-shopping once, and at the beach when the guys had the kids in the water—we'd gotten along perfectly well. Matt loved her, so we did.

There it was again, that loyalty, even if it was

more of an effort than a given. And I didn't want it to be an effort for anyone to love Michael.

Keeping Drew a secret wouldn't be possible, of course. Not in my family, or in Michael's. Especially Michael's—how would his mother react to the news that she had another grandchild? And his sister? They were blood, if that mattered to them. And what if Drew asked to meet them?

No, we had to tell them, and we would. But the cloak of denial felt so good, a coat on a cold, windy day, and removing it was going to sting. Not today. Soon, but not today.

The boys skidded into the room, both slightly sweaty, in bare feet now. Owen sported a jagged streak of dirt on one cheek.

Robin heaved a sigh as she herded them toward the bathroom. "Wash up, guys. This isn't a picnic."

"It's not a bad idea, though," Jack said, appearing in the doorway, just as flushed as the kids. He'd obviously been chasing them around the yard, and my mother gave him a fond smile as she carried in the garden salad and a plate of warm rolls.

The next few minutes were the usual chaos, as everyone found seats and began passing plates amid a jumble of voices and laughter and the occasional protest from the card table, where Eli and Owen were seated. My mother and I made at least half a dozen trips back to the kitchen, for pepper, more napkins, a new glass of milk for Eli, another serving spoon, and I didn't have even a moment to gauge Emma's mood. She'd followed Michael into the dining room without a word and taken a chair next to my father, and a stab of concern pierced my calm when I sat down next to Michael and noticed Emma's head bent toward Dad in conversation.

Michael laid a hand on my thigh beneath the table, his fingers warm and solid through my linen pants, and for a moment I leaned into him, letting our shoulders bump.

"Relax," he murmured, and I had to restrain myself from rolling my eyes. Beside me he was strung taut, and the purplish smudges under his eyes were a giveaway that he hadn't been sleeping well.

I hated this, all of it. Telling myself the meal was almost over, right here at my parents' table—and on my father's birthday. Avoiding my mother, when I usually talked to her on the phone every day. She'd called me yesterday, wondering if we were still coming to Dad's birthday lunch, and I'd hung up the phone miserable, like a teenager who knows she's about to get caught smoking or cutting class any day.

I helped myself to some of the vegetable frittata Robin had brought, as the conversation swirled around me. Jack and my father were arguing about baseball, something about the designated hitter, and my mother was quizzing Eli about school. Robin asked Michael's mother about the trip she was planning to Ireland, and Maureen shook her head at the price of airfare. I sat back, watching Michael pick at his chicken salad, his eyes on his plate, and then looked at Emma again.

Teenagers could always eat. She was still upset. It was in the set of her shoulders, the curtain of hair she'd allowed to fall over her face, even the clothes she'd chosen, an old white button-down over faded jeans. She'd forgone makeup today, and her only jewelry was a pair of plain silver hoops she'd gotten for her birthday a few years earlier. But she was forking up chicken salad and some of my mother's macerated raspberries, working her way toward the roll she'd slathered with butter.

At least she wouldn't starve.

She glanced up when she felt my eyes on her, and I tried a smile. She wasn't having it. Stabbing another chunk of chicken with her fork, she lowered her gaze, her mouth tight. Right then, I would have sold my soul to go back to the days when reconciliation could be bought with an ice-cream cone or the trillionth rental of a Mary-Kate and Ashley video.

"Tess? You are coming, aren't you?"

I forced my attention back to the table, where my mother was staring at me with a frown.

"Coming where?" I said, moving food around on my plate before I got scolded for not eating.

"Next weekend, the barbecue. Nell wants to discuss the wedding plans and show us some pictures of dresses for you and Liza. She's going to come, too."

Liza was Nell's best friend, and her other bridesmaid. Shit. She'd be driving all the way from Connecticut, and I hadn't even told Nell that I wouldn't be around. I hadn't told anybody, and they had no reason to suspect it, since Michael and I never went anywhere but to my parents' house over the holiday weekend.

And yet, that Mom had made it a question rather than a statement was already proof she understood something was up. The woman was preternatural about some things, and reading her kids had always been one of them. She set down her glass of iced tea as I glanced back at Emma.

She'd straightened up, blinking, her fork suspended over her plate, and her eyes were brighter than they'd been all day. Michael cleared his throat as I sent her a warning glare, but Emma was too quick.

"We won't be here next week, Nana," she said, and the nearly vicious satisfaction in her tone resounded like a slap.

"Tess?" Dad was building another sandwich, shoveling chicken salad into a roll. His expression was only mildly curious, but I knew my mother felt the tension. Her face had closed up like a flower after dark.

"We do have other plans next week, Mom," I said. I sounded calm—that was good. The paper napkin in my lap had already been shredded into pieces.

"Tell them where, Mom," Emma said, letting her fork clatter to her empty plate. "Or maybe Dad should."

Oh God.

"This isn't the time or the place, Emma," Michael said, and I cringed. His voice was actually shaking. Everyone had a breaking point, and I was pretty sure he'd just reached his.

"Michael, what's wrong?" his mother asked. She inched forward, her lips working soundlessly for a moment. "Is everyone all right? Is someone…sick?"

"Mom, it's fine, really." Michael took a deep breath and stood. The silence was alive, thrumming with electricity. This was not the usual family lunch, not by a long shot. Even the boys were quiet, staring wide-eyed at the grown-up drama. "Emma, why don't you join me in the kitchen."

She surprised me then. She had her breaking point, too. But something in the air had gotten into her—the audience maybe, or her own sense of righteous indignation. Her chin was up when she said, clear and firm, "No."

Robin stood up suddenly. "I'll just get the boys some more—" she began, but Emma cut her off.

"No, wait, Aunt Robin," she said, crossing her arms over her chest. "Don't you want to know why we're not going to be at the party next week?"

I was still finding my voice when my mother said, "Emma, you're being unbelievably rude."

"I don't care," Emma shot back, and then she was on her feet, too, ready for flight as soon as she aimed her next barbs. I froze, waiting for them—there was no stopping this now, and part of me was almost relieved. A few words and at least the news would be out, even if the repercussions were bound to reverberate for a while.

Michael had frozen, too, and I fumbled for his hand as Emma's throat worked compulsively.

"We have to go to Cambridge next weekend,"

she said, when her tears began. I was vaguely aware that my own were right behind them. "And you know why? You're never going to believe it. It's like the stupid Springer show or something." She flicked my father's steadying hand away from her arm and took another breath.

Michael didn't let her finish. I closed my eyes as he opened his mouth, one hand held up to silence Emma. I clung to his other hand, so hard I was afraid I'd broken the skin with my nails. But his voice was steady when he said, "We're going to Cambridge to meet my son."

CHAPTER SEVEN

I WISH I COULD SAY THAT Michael's relationship with Sophia, and therefore Drew's existence, was all Jackson Devic's fault, since it started with him. But that would be the coward's way out. In the end, Jackson wasn't the one who decided I should end things with Michael. That was my decision.

I borrowed Nell's battered little Civic to drive up and visit Michael in March of my junior year. The train would have been more sensible—the forecasters were predicting snow up and down the East Coast, and I wasn't used to driving anymore, living in the city. But I wanted to be alone. I wanted to crank music and smoke cigarettes, which I'd taken up again in the past few months, even though I'd never smoked during all the time I'd spent at ballet school, where everyone smoked incessantly to keep from eating.

The cigarettes were a by-product of stress. I

was edgy, itchy, restless, and had been all fall. I needed something to do, something to hold on to, something to keep me from screaming, which was what I really longed to do.

And the reason for that was Jackson Devic. There was no denying it.

I'd been working for him since late September, and since October I'd been sick to my stomach, and sick at heart. Jackson was my boss, as well as a divorced man nearly twice my age, but it didn't matter. Like Cyrus, he fascinated me, and I knew—or believed—he shouldn't.

Michael and I were completely happy, despite the geographic distance between us. There were the summers, of course, and the long winter breaks, and phone bills we'd be paying off until the end of time. We'd grown into the huge, sometimes frightening feelings that had consumed us when we first met. And the miles didn't matter—we were connected where it connected.

Or so I thought. And then I met Jackson.

He was a photographer with a studio in Chelsea, and in September of my junior year I had answered his ad in the *Village Voice* for an assistant.

A Winston hung from the corner of his lips as he scanned the book of photos I'd brought with me. He squinted when the smoke curled up past his stubbled jaw, and a moment later flicked the butt into an overflowing ashtray on the worktable where he was balanced, one narrow hip on the edge.

"Not many photos here." His tone was curt, flat, and his gray eyes were the same color as the smoke.

"I only started last year," I pointed out, hoping he wouldn't notice me twisting my hands into a knot beneath the surface of the table. "I was a dancer all through high school, and I had planned to dance instead of going to college."

"What happened?" He'd flipped back to the first pictures in the book, the shots I'd taken of graffiti all over the city.

I shrugged in my best imitation of a bored, blasé college girl. "I smashed up my knee. By the time the surgery and physical therapy were over, I would have been starting from scratch."

"You're at NYU?" He glanced up and raked a hand over the salt-and-pepper hair cropped dangerously close to his head. "Majoring in photography?"

I nodded. For no good reason, my heart was hammering, and I could feel the buzz of adrenaline in my veins. Getting into the program hadn't been easy, but never once had I been this nervous during the whole process.

Jackson's photos were everywhere in the crowded little space, tacked to raw corkboard, enlarged and framed, stacked in contact sheets on the worktable, taped to the brick wall at the far end of the room. And they were magnificent. Everything I loved about photography was evident in his pictures—perspective, shadow, lighting, color saturation, tinting, angles and fades and effects. My professors were brilliant, for the most part, but Jackson Devic was the real thing, a working photographer. Jackson could teach me the truth about what I could make a camera do, and more—the disappointments and the screw-ups and the secrets about working as a photographer that no one ever bothered to include in a lecture.

And I was sure Jackson knew all of them.

The studio was a man's space through and through, coated in a fine film of dust, with empty disposable cups and crushed cigarette packs littering the floor and overflowing the wastebaskets. Music played in the background, something strangely bluesy and mournful; a forgotten pair of jeans was draped over the radiator underneath the window, and a dozen white roses had died in a plain glass vase, their shriveled, brittle petals scattered over the surface of another table.

"Dancing is a long way from taking pictures," Jackson said, considering me as he lit another cigarette, striking a wooden match against the wood.

He wasn't wrong. Photography was about as different from ballet as anything could be, outside of statistics or dead languages, but a camera felt as natural in my hands as my pointe shoes had once felt on my feet. Both visual art forms, yes, but photography allowed me to be outside the art I was creating—when I was dancing, I could only feel the way I appeared onstage, the effect I made. When I thought of the early-childhood-education major I had declared in desperation at the beginning of my sophomore year, it was hard not to laugh.

"I had a course last year," I explained, and reached out to point to the graffiti pictures again. "Modern art. It was just an elective, and I only took it because it fit into my schedule, but one of the things we could do for the final was a photo essay. I borrowed a friend's camera, and I realized…"

The words dried up in my throat. What was I going to tell him? That I'd fallen in love? I had, but it would sound trite, impossibly childish and romantic.

"You liked it," Jackson said, instead, and for the first time since I'd walked into the studio, there was the hint of a smile on his lips. "You're talented, too. Inexperienced, but you've got an eye. That's a good thing, as I'm sure all your professors have told you."

I nodded, my cheeks hot with pleasure. Even now I don't know whether I was more thrilled that he thought I had talent or that his tone had skidded just up to the edge of contempt when he said "professors."

I began work the next day, and within two weeks I was spending most of my free time either at Jackson's studio or out with him on shoots. He picked up all kinds of assignments— stringing for the newspapers, a lot of editorial work, the occasional portrait. "I'm an equal-opportunity photographer," he would say with that same not-quite smile as he packed equipment into one of his bags.

He was teaching me to be the same kind of photographer, whether he meant to or not, and over the next few months I learned dozens of other things from him—the nuances of film brands and speeds, favored lenses, developing techniques, lighting tricks. But I was also learning the meaning of confusion. Curiosity seemed to have very sharp teeth, because it was gnawing through my certainty that Michael and I were meant to be together.

My infatuation with Cyrus, during freshman year, had ended nearly as soon as it had begun. Everything had been new that year, and the glimpses of other lives, other paths, other choices had been overwhelming. Cyrus's laidback charm had been appealing at a time when I was confused about what I wanted, not only from college but from my life, when I was overwhelmed by how easily and how deeply Michael seemed to love me, when most of the time I didn't feel I deserved it.

I loved Michael. I did. But somehow that fall I had begun to resent him and everything he meant to me. In Jackson's company the comfort of imagining my life neatly mapped out in front of me—college, photography, marriage to Michael, kids, a home—had begun to seem like a vise, instead.

A vise that meant I would never know if I had chosen right. If I was supposed to be with Michael, or if I was ignoring other paths—one with Jackson Devic at the end of it, for instance.

I can see it all now so clearly. I had a ridiculous schoolgirl crush on Jackson, a combination of idol worship, old-fashioned lust and an ego-stroking that felt too exhilarating to ignore. And Jackson was so good at his particular style of stroking. I was the teacher's pet, no question, and I blithely wrote off the fact that I was the only pupil.

Jackson encouraged me, praised my eye and my style, and when he chastised me for laziness or poor composition, the implied meaning was that I could do better, that he wouldn't stand for me wasting my talent. I could have spent every minute in that smoky, gritty studio above West Twenty-second Street, with Jackson's Johnny Cash records spinning in the background, jittery with stale coffee and the electric rush of possibility.

He took me to a coffee shop way over on Eleventh Avenue one night after a photo shoot. It had begun to rain, a chilly gray drizzle, and inside the diner the dull, greasy windows had steamed up. He slid into the booth in the back corner, shaking raindrops from his closely shorn head, and shrugged off his navy peacoat.

We ordered coffee and pie, and I babbled as I made notes on the shoot, an editorial piece for *Mademoiselle*. Jackson had let me take a roll of film myself, and I was high with the excitement of it.

"Come back to the studio," he said when the waitress had bussed away our cups and slapped the check on the table. "Come back with me now."

For a moment that seemed endless, everything stopped—the clatter of dishes in the kitchen, the noisy conversation in the next booth, the whisper of tires on the wet pavement outside. The distance between us, not even three feet across the scarred Formica tabletop, closed up until I swore I could see each of his eyelashes individually, feel his breath against my cheek, hear the muffled thump of his heart.

He was asking me to sleep with him. I'd imagined it, dreamed about it, but until now I hadn't really believed it would happen. There was safety in that—fantasizing wasn't cheating, after all. But the moment I let Jackson kiss me…

My ears were still ringing with the rush of adrenaline when he leaned across the table and added, "I want to develop your film right now. I want to see what you did."

Turns out that relief and humiliation can actually coexist, with room left over for an unexpected jolt of pride. I couldn't do anything but nod at him as he pulled out his wallet to pay the check.

But I wasn't completely wrong. He touched me too often, in too many different ways, his shoulder bumping mine here, his hand on the small of my back there. Once that night, when the contact sheet of my photographs emerged from the tray, he slung his arm around my shoulders and kissed me on the forehead. His lips were warm and firm, and his nearness was intoxicating, the dusky scents of smoke and coffee and damp wool so new. So unlike Michael.

I didn't decide to leave Michael that night. But the seed was planted and over the next few months it took root until it flowered into something poisonous. I hadn't done anything wrong, but I'd wanted to, and in my heart that was enough to condemn me. In ballet, every ending is either tragic or perfect, death or bliss. Michael was my hero, and he loved me so completely, I was at fault even for wondering what my life would become without him.

Which meant I didn't deserve his love.

That was what I had convinced myself as I drove to Cambridge that late winter day, the radio blaring and the window cracked as I smoked cigarette after cigarette. Nell was going to kill me for it, but I didn't care. I couldn't quite imagine the moments after I told Michael that we should break up. The rest of my life was a blank.

I drove three hundred miles of highway that day, and the only thing I could picture was Michael's face.

WATCHING MICHAEL THE SATURDAY morning we were leaving for Massachusetts, as he loaded the trunk of the Volvo with our few weekend bags, I could remember that long-ago Michael so clearly. He was thinner now, just beginning to go gray at the temples, and the angles of his face were more sharply defined, but his expression was so similar to the one he'd given me that day in his stuffy little apartment in Cambridge, my throat choked with emotion.

His eyes had always been his giveaway. But I could read so much more in the set of his jaw this morning, the omnipresent dark smudges under his eyes that proved my suspicion he hadn't slept last night. As he slung his overnight bag into the trunk, he glanced up and noticed me on the steps. His attempt at a smile was pathetic as he took the duffel bag I'd dropped at my feet.

"I hope you're caffeinated," I said lightly, holding up a cup of coffee. "Because it's a long trip."

"You can drive if you like." He slammed the trunk shut and joined me on the steps. "Did you see Emma?"

I rolled my eyes and wound my arm around him as we went inside. She'd been curled on the sofa earlier, her iPod already on, her bag beside her and her best sullen-teenager expression pasted to her face. "How did you get her to pack?"

"I threatened to do it for her." He shrugged and rinsed out his coffee cup in the sink. "I hope making her come isn't a mistake."

I fought back a frustrated sigh. "It's too late to do anything about it now. And to tell you the truth, I'd rather have her sniping at us all weekend than endlessly rehashing this with my parents or your mom. Again."

He stared at me for a moment before he walked into the living room, and I winced. *Way to go, Tess,* I admonished myself. *As if he's not tense enough already.*

All week the scene at my parents' last Sunday had hovered in the house like a foul smell. Getting through it the first time had been hard enough—discussing it would have done nothing but upset us both.

And really, what was there to discuss? That the stunned silence at the table had rung like struck glass, that Emma had burst into noisy tears moments later, that Michael's mother had actually shouted at her before Robin hustled the boys out to the backyard, their eyes huge and their cheeks hot with the excitement of the adult drama at the table?

Everyone was entitled to a reaction, as we'd

learned so quickly with Emma. It didn't change the fact that Drew existed, and that he was Michael's son.

But it didn't mean that I wanted our history dissected and analyzed by my whole family, either. Hell, *I* didn't even want to dissect it. Because I was the one who'd pushed Michael away that horrible day in Cambridge. I was the one who'd watched him cry, who'd listened to him arguing that I could have space if I needed it, that he loved me, he would never stop loving me…

And Michael knew it. Michael knew that I was partly to blame for everything that had happened, and what was more, he understood that the worst part of me hated the thought that Emma and our families would figure that out.

I drained the last of my coffee, savoring its burn in my throat, and put my cup in the sink next to Michael's. God, I couldn't even think about that day, still. I had never felt smaller, more selfish, stupider.

But I couldn't forget driving home the next morning, and the awful sense of freedom that had made me turn the radio up higher and sing along to Springsteen and The Cure at the top of my lungs, even as tears slid down my face.

Loving someone is a huge responsibility. And

that day, I had shrugged off the burden, grateful for the loss of its weight.

Michael appeared in the doorway to the kitchen with Emma beside him, and without speaking any more than necessary, we hustled Emma into the car with Walter—we were dropping him off at my parents' house for the weekend. My mother met me at the door, still wrapped in her cotton bathrobe, her gray bob uncombed, and I felt a sharp pinch of guilt when I noticed the lines around her eyes. For the first time, it hit me that she was getting older.

It was worry, and I knew she worried out of love. But I couldn't quite erase the memory of the shock on her face when Michael had made his announcement, and the way she'd whispered, "Were you unfaithful to Tess?"

As if her heart was breaking. As if I wasn't to blame. As if I were the innocent party.

"Hi, Mom," I said now, leading Walter into the house. His tail wagged furiously, and he slathered her hands with doggy affection when she leaned forward to pet his head.

"You'll be back on Monday night?" she asked accepting the bag of dog food and then unhooking Walter's leash. She was so obviously not meeting my eyes she might as well have announced it.

"If not sooner." That I could keep my tone so light, so casual, as if I was anticipating nothing more serious than a carefree holiday weekend away with my family, was amazing. "Don't forget to give Walter one of the good biscuits after he's pooped. He'll sulk otherwise."

I kissed her cheek as I turned toward the door, and she grabbed my forearm, confusion and concern and something like grief in her eyes. "You're okay, honey? Really?"

If she started to cry, I would cry. And if I went out to the car crying, then Michael would either cry or scream or possibly throw something. God knows what Emma would do. I was so sick of tears. I couldn't believe that I had any left.

"Mom, I'm fine." I tugged my arm out of her grasp and hugged her, breathing in the familiar scent of her Chanel, pressing my cheek to her cool one. "We're fine. Or we will be. I promise."

But the three of us sat in that car for hours on the way to Massachusetts without saying a word.

CHAPTER EIGHT

We walked into Charlie's kitchen at just after one, rushed and edgy. After battling traffic as we neared Boston, Michael had called Drew on his cell to let him know we were close to Cambridge. We hadn't even checked into our hotel yet, a consequence Michael had predicted when we stopped for coffee and doughnuts on the way out of town that morning. All of us were rumpled and stiff from hours in the car, and the tension in the air around us was probably tangible from a mile away.

"It's not a big deal, Michael," I said as we made our way down Brattle Street in the hazy sunshine. "We just drove six hours. I'm sure he can forgive us being thirty minutes late."

Michael didn't reply, and he didn't really need to. He wasn't angry that we were late, of course. He was nervous and unsure of what the hell we were doing, and I didn't blame him. I felt exactly the same way, with a side of guilty resentment.

And a frightening itch to smack my daughter, who had perfected her pout and was practically oozing outraged dignity.

I grabbed her arm as Michael opened the door to the restaurant, a Cambridge institution we'd eaten at plenty of times when I'd visited him. "I am expecting you to behave like a grown-up, Emma. I know you're not one, and I know this is hugely upsetting and...well, weird, but don't make it worse. Got it?"

Harsh words, but just a minute away from meeting Michael's son, there on the sidewalk, neon beer signs lit up in the window and college students walking past in pairs, laughing and arguing, I was too freaked out to care. Emma simply nodded, bright, hot spots of color in her cheeks, her eyes wide, and we followed her father inside.

Drew was standing inside the door. He didn't need an introduction or a name tag—I would have recognized him anywhere. He looked just the way Michael had at his age, and the shock of it literally knocked the air from my lungs for a second.

I don't know what I was expecting. DNA doesn't lie, and Drew had half of Michael's. It was all over him, in his lanky frame and the huge dark eyes fringed with impossibly long lashes, the dark hair falling over his forehead, the familiar curve of his bottom lip, softer than a boy's had any right to be.

But there was more—the intelligence in his eyes shadowed with uncertainty, the intensity in the way he stood, hands jammed in the pockets of his jeans, shoulders stiff.

For a moment, all I could register was that he looked so unsure, so pale with worry, that I was tempted to hug him.

A few steps ahead of me, Michael had stopped dead. The restaurant was crowded and noisy, with the jukebox going and a knot of customers at the long bar arguing over the Red Sox game. It was the wrong place, I realized suddenly, the wrong time. The place smelled of onion rings and beer and too many people. We should have picked somewhere private, somewhere much quieter, but even as I stood panicked, Michael said, "Drew?" and reached out to shake his son's hand.

Behind me Emma made some kind of a noise—her bottom lip was caught between her teeth and her arms were folded over her chest. Holding something in, which was fine with me. I was having enough trouble keeping my own eyes from spilling tears. The moment had the surreal quality of the kind of TV movie everyone had seen a million times—a touching family reunion! Cut to artful tears and the group smiling over cheeseburgers!

"Michael." Drew shook his hand vigorously, the hard set of his jaw finally relaxing, and the two of them simply stared at each other.

I swallowed hard as I moved aside to let a man who'd walked in get by. Women would have hugged, I thought absently. Men were so strange. Michael and Drew were father and son, after all. But what did that mean, really, when they'd never met before today?

Michael broke the silence, turning to me and Emma. "Drew, this is Tess, my wife. And this is Emma, our daughter."

Drew's hand was warm and firm, his fingers shaped disconcertingly like Michael's. *Before and after. Version 1.0 and version 2.0.* I had to swallow back a gust of laughter that would have verged on hysteria.

"I'm so happy to meet you," Drew said, and I managed a smile and a nod. Emma wasn't doing much better—she looked almost starstruck, her eyes huge and glassy. At least she wasn't pouting.

"Our booth should be ready," Drew went on. "I know one of the waiters."

Michael's smile was sudden, and full of relief. Drew was sweet and polite and smart— a nice kid. It was the one thing I hadn't doubted.

For a meal that could have been tense and awkward, lunch was surprisingly pleasant. Emma and I ordered the famous lobster rolls, and Michael had a cheeseburger dripping with grease, and fat, hot steak fries on the side. But Drew only picked at a salad and a cup of soup, which struck me as strange. It was nearly June for one thing, and he was a twenty-year-old boy. At that age, my brothers and Michael could have—and most likely would have— eaten a *double* cheeseburger, with a shake, fries and maybe even onion rings. And dessert.

But the longer we lingered at the booth upstairs, comfortably ranged by gender across the table—Michael seated with Drew, Emma and me opposite them—the more unavoidable was my conclusion. Drew was far too pale for a kid his age, even one who didn't spend a lot of time outdoors. And his complexion wasn't simply pale; it had a faint blue translucence. The circles under his eyes were purple and every once in a while he seemed a little out of breath.

He's weak, the mother part of me whispered. *Sick. Really, really sick.* Not that I could ask, of course—Michael and Drew were helming the conversation, and Drew had insisted nearly as soon as we were seated with our menus that he had wanted to meet Michael out of curiosity.

Maybe it was true, but it wasn't curiosity alone. I knew it, in the same wordless place in my gut that clutched when Emma was lying to me, or when she was upset about something too big for her to handle by herself.

Apparently, my maternal instinct worked whether the child in question was mine by blood or not.

"So you're studying architecture?" Michael said now, biting into his enormous cheeseburger and obviously oblivious that Drew had barely eaten a thing. "I can't come up with a better place than MIT to do that."

"Yeah, MIT is pretty awesome." Drew glanced up through those thick lashes, an apology in his eyes. "I considered Harvard for a while, though."

Michael sputtered iced tea, and wiped his mouth with his napkin. "Just because I went to Harvard… I mean, if that's why you thought about it…"

Drew glanced up at Emma, who had frozen, a French fry snagged from her father's plate halfway to her lips. "Um, well, I kind of meant I thought about it because it's such a good school, but I didn't actually know you went there until…" He trailed off, miserable, and focused on the uneaten chowder in his bowl.

I was waiting for Michael to reassure him, when Emma blurted out, "Where did your mom go? Didn't she go to Harvard?"

The pink elephant that had hovered silently over the table, so far not remarked upon, landed with a nearly audible crash.

This time it was me Drew glanced at, and I saw the same wordless apology in his eyes. How much had Sophia told him about her relationship with Michael? About Michael's relationship with me?

"My mom went to Boston University." Drew shrugged. "She and—" He stopped short and colored.

I'll give him this—he caught himself in time, or close enough. I could guess what he had been going to say. Sophia and Michael had met because they lived in the same apartment building. Michael had already explained it all to me, more than I wanted to know, but this afternoon didn't need to be weirder for Emma than it already was. I had no interest in her getting the lowdown on Daddy's romance with her half brother's mom.

God, it *was* almost like something out of *The Jerry Springer Show*.

Drew was covering his mistake, rushing on to say, "Mom was all for me going wherever was best. And MIT is an excellent school for any kind of technology or science. What do you think you'll major in, Emma?"

Michael met my eyes with a little smile at that, and sat back in the red leather booth. The kid was definitely bright. There was no better way to distract a teenage girl than to ask her to talk about herself.

Emma played coy for a minute or two, giving one-word answers to Drew's questions, but she seemed grateful for the attention. Half brother or not, it wasn't every day a cute college boy talked to her, especially one who didn't treat her like an irritating child. By the time I'd finished my iced tea and the rest of Michael's fries, he'd managed to charm her into giving him details about the school play and her part in it.

The waitress arrived with the check, and Michael pulled out his wallet as Emma and I tidied up our side of the table. Drew opened his mouth, but Michael cut him off before he got a word out.

"It's on me. My pleasure," he said, and Drew smiled.

"Thanks…Michael."

Would it ever not be awkward? Would Drew call Michael "Dad" at some point? Did Michael want him to? Was this low-key lunch it, the answer to Drew's curiosity and Michael's sense of obligation? As quickly as it had disappeared, the tension was back, a tight fist in my muscles and shoulders.

And it would only get worse, I realized. Because Drew took Michael aside out in the sultry afternoon sunshine and asked if he and Michael could talk alone for a while. I had no problem with that, especially if it meant Drew would tell Michael the whole truth about why he'd contacted him. There was no polite way to veto Drew's plan for Emma and me while the guys wandered through Cambridge.

"I already asked Mom," Drew said, shrugging those painfully bony shoulders at me, with eyes too much like Michael's, full of hope and uncertainty. "She said you and Emma were welcome to hang out there for the afternoon, and then she'd love it if you could all stay for dinner."

The fist clenched harder, tightening viciously at the base of my skull. Meet Sophia, with Emma as some kind of bizarre chaperone? I couldn't think of an idea I hated more. But I nodded, and flashed my best imitation of a smile as I lied. "That sounds great."

SOPHIA WAS CARRYING GROCERY bags up the front steps of an old three-story frame house when Emma and I arrived at Walden Street, slightly winded. The walk in the soft late-spring sun was a much longer one than I'd expected— so much longer that I hadn't had to drag it out the way I'd planned.

I had been anticipating a moment to compose myself, to meet Drew's mother for the first time, smile in place after waiting on the other side of a closed door. But there she was, chin-length dark hair swinging around her face, arms full of brown bags.

"You found it." Sophia's expression didn't give anything away—if she was uncomfortable meeting the wife and daughter of the man who had fathered her son, it didn't show. Her eyes were a clear brown. "And here I am not even in the house yet. Come on in."

"I can carry one of those," Emma offered, running up the broad gray steps to the little porch. I fought back a frown. Emma usually never helped with chores until I ticked off the many things she wouldn't be able to do without her allowance.

"Thanks," Sophia said. "It's Emma, right? We're on the second floor."

Emma nodded as she accepted a stuffed grocery bag and opened the screen door, and I started up the steps as I said, "And I'm Tess. Hi."

"Hi, Tess." Sophia stuck out her free hand—she had a surprisingly strong grasp, and her gaze never wavered as she smiled at me. The flicker of uncertainty I'd heard on the phone last week was gone. Home-field advantage, I decided. Not that it was a contest, and certainly not a battle. I had to keep that in mind. Hell, I needed to get a grip. "Come on in."

The smell hit me as I followed her up the stairs to the second floor—oil paint and what I thought was turpentine. And there was Drew the moment I walked through the door into a narrow hallway—a three-year-old Drew, curled into an overstuffed sofa, fast asleep.

"Did you paint this?" Emma asked, saving me the trouble. She had put down the grocery bag somewhere, and was standing in front of the painting, one careful finger tracing a brush-stroke on the bottom edge of the red sofa.

"Guilty," Sophia said lightly, and continued down the hall, before disappearing into a room to the right. The hall was lined with paintings, I realized, all in the same rich, saturated colors, all obviously painted by the same hand.

It might have been the hall at my own house had the paintings been replaced with photographs.

Sophia stuck her head through the doorway

a moment later. "Come on in the kitchen. I have iced tea."

Emma didn't even spare a backward glance for me—she examined each painting as she headed for the kitchen, stripping off her iPod headphones as she went. If I'd imagined her awkward and resentful in Sophia's presence I'd been wrong, and now I didn't know if I was more anxious that she was playing up to Sophia simply to push my buttons, or if her fascination with the woman was as genuine as it seemed.

"I get paid to teach Italian," Sophia explained as Emma and I sat down at a cozy oak table in the corner of the kitchen. The sun up here on the second floor was fantastic, especially on this side of the house. The kitchen was flooded with warm gold light, making the bright yellow walls buttery. "But I'm a painter at heart. Just a… realistic one, I guess. Even before I had Drew, I didn't have much interest in doing the starving-artist thing."

The soul of an artist was all over the apartment, I discovered later, when Sophia had set Emma up on the small back porch with a small easel and some paint to fool around with. It was in the colors on the walls, the way the apartment's edges had been blunted with fabric or pillows, the patterned rugs that masked the humble origins of the wood floors, the trompe l'oeil skyline painted on one wall of Drew's childhood bedroom.

What was also evident was a sense of content-ment, and a kind of assuredness. This was a home, and a happy one, not a way station before traveling to another life, a bigger house. Those qualities alone answered a myriad of questions, but I couldn't help asking myself if Sophia had ever regretted leaving Michael in the dark about their son, or wondered if they could have made a life together.

Because I could so clearly see everything about this woman that had attracted my husband. Especially all those years ago, with me throwing what amounted to a teenage tantrum of sorts. Sophia was a few years older than Michael, and aside from being damnably sensual, she had probably been just as confident then as she was now. Majoring in Italian to ensure an income even when painting was her passion. Living on her own, already beyond roommates and keg parties and ridiculous fits of identity crisis.

We'd ended up in the living room, tucked into either end of the same comfy sofa in the painting, and as I sipped my iced tea, I realized the first awkward silence had fallen between us.

Not my fault, I told myself with all the maturity of a kindergartner, fixing my stare on a self-portrait of a younger Sophia. That was the last thing I wanted to notice, of course, but it was too late—I couldn't bring myself to meet her eyes.

Sophia broke the silence as she set her glass on the coffee table and tucked her bare feet onto the sofa. "I know you might have questions."

Another understatement. I had questions, all right, but I wasn't sure I was ready for answers to any of them. Except one.

I swallowed and faced her. "Can you tell me why Drew decided to contact Michael now? I mean, would it be…?"

"Betraying him?" Her smile was lopsided, and more than a little halfhearted. "Maybe. But I'm sure he's telling Michael now, and I know Michael will tell you."

So there was a reason beyond simple curiosity. Judging by the flash of fear and grief in Sophia's eyes, it wasn't a good one.

"He's sick, Tess," she said, and her voice broke a little. *With the weight of worry,* I thought absently, even as my heartbeat stuttered. *The burden of secrets.*

"How sick?"

It was Emma, in the doorway, a smear of red paint across one cheek, her hands splattered with the results of her painting experiment. Her face was blank, but I could read the shock in her eyes even from a distance.

Sophia glanced at me, and I nodded. We would all know soon enough, and we would all have to deal with it, whatever it was. I had simply never imagined that the cozy little "we" that had always been Michael, Emma and me would include two other people.

"He has what's called acute lymphoblastic leukemia." The words were too big, too foreign, even though they sounded eerily comfortable on Sophia's tongue. She picked at a loose fringe on the hem of her jeans as she spoke, and her voice was the only sound in the room.

"He's dying."

CHAPTER NINE

I PLAYED THE WORDS OVER AND over in my head the next day, as we drove home through a chain of early thunderstorms. Michael had suggested we go home instead of staying another day, so we could talk things through and make arrangements, and I for one hadn't argued. I longed for my own house, my own bed, and was seriously considering staying there all day Monday, huddled under the covers.

The windshield wipers slapped the glass in rhythm as we sped down the I-95, echoing the words I hadn't been able to forget all night. *Bone marrow donor.* No matter how I attempted to think rationally about the procedures Sophia and Drew had explained, the words were sharp and ugly, as gruesome as needles, and just as painful.

Emma had burst into tears over the simple lemon pasta Sophia had made for dinner, and run out of the room. The door to the bathroom had slammed a moment later, but before I could get up, Drew had held up his hand. "Let me," he'd said, his own eyes glassy. "If she understands it's not so scary for me…"

If Sophia's tight face was anything to judge by, this was a patent lie, but I let him go to her. A brother comforting his sister, I thought, and turned to see Michael's shoulders hunched into turtle mode. You couldn't grieve for something you'd never known you had, but Michael was faced now with what he'd missed. And there was every chance he would lose it again all too soon.

We'd talked late into the night, once we'd checked into the hotel and Emma was in bed with the TV glowing blue on the dresser and her headphones on. She'd watched the silent images on the screen for a half hour or so, listening to whatever music was shuffled up, until her eyelids finally drifted shut and she fell asleep.

There was no question that we would do whatever we could to help Drew. As I lay curled against Michael's chest on the stiff hotel mattress, he confided everything Drew had told him that afternoon in a coffee shop not far from Sophia's apartment, the early symptoms, the diagnosis, the chemotherapy.

The fear that the leukemia might have come from his side of the family, somehow, that our own gorgeous, healthy Emma might be facing the same fate one day, went unspoken. Voicing the fears would make them too real, and far too possible.

"Drew's such a good kid," Michael murmured as he stroked my hair. "Smart, you know? With a good heart. He has a *future,* damn it. Or he would, if he wasn't sick. It's just so goddamn unfair. It proves every cliché in the book, too. You never believe something like this will happen to you, you know? Or someone you care about. And it always seems to happen to someone who doesn't deserve it. Why aren't the serial killers out there getting leukemia, for God's sake?"

I didn't have an answer for that—no one did. But when he asked how I felt about his returning to Cambridge in the coming week to undergo testing to determine whether he was a bone marrow match, I didn't hesitate. No matter what had happened between Michael and me all those years ago, no matter what had led to Drew's conception, he was Michael's child. Sophia had shouldered the burden of parenting him alone for all these years—the very least we could do was offer any kind of help we could to give Drew a shot at surviving.

Even if that meant that the carefree summer I had envisioned for us was going to become a

flurry of trips between home and Massachusetts, with the bonus of medical tests and procedures. Even if it meant, in the back of my
mind, that I would wonder if Emma might be
considered a possible donor, too.

I shifted to get more comfortable as we
crossed the line between Connecticut and New
York. Michael had been silent for the past hour,
listening to an R.E.M. CD, and Emma was
asleep in the back seat. Her book had tumbled
off her lap onto the floor, and her half-empty
bottle of Diet Pepsi rolled back and forth as the
car moved. I was being selfish, even if it was
secretly. No, I didn't want Drew to die—even
if he hadn't been Michael's son, I wouldn't
want that. But I hated the idea of Michael
undergoing anything painful, and I hated the
idea of losing him this summer to the car, Cambridge, Drew's cancer—to a son I had only the
most peripheral part in creating, a young man
I didn't know, and maybe never would.

I longed for Michael to talk to me. And what
I wanted him to say was, *I'm sorry, I never
should have slept with Sophia, and I know
exactly how much you love me, even if twenty
years ago you broke up with me because you
were attracted to another man and scared of
commitment.*

Not likely. Ridiculous, in fact. Stupid. But realizing that didn't keep me from wishing he would say those things. And it definitely didn't stop me from feeling guilty about wanting him to at the same time.

Michael had too much on his mind to comfort me in the here and now, and my memories weren't any help, either. I couldn't stop mulling over the months Michael and I had spent apart. He'd never told me how he spent them, and now I had just enough information to drive myself crazy with. He hadn't been alone. I knew that now, at least—as much as it hurt.

The rain never stopped, and I spent the rest of the drive listening to the wheels shushing on the pavement, and pretending to be asleep.

"You going to eat that?"

Sometime early in the summer, Jackson and I were in his studio after a day spent developing film from one of the rare weddings he agreed to photograph. He'd ordered in Chinese when we noticed it was after seven—neither of us had eaten since noon. My egg roll sat untouched on my plate as I sorted through the proofs.

"You can have it," I said. Jackson's appetite was inhuman. He'd already plowed through a pint of pork-fried rice and an order of Hunan beef.

"Great picture of the flower girl." I held up a shot of the five-year-old in her pink dress, petals fluttering to the ground as she traipsed up the aisle.

"It's not tough to get a good picture of a pretty girl." He bit through the egg roll, then tossed it onto his own plate and reached for the old Nikon on the table beside him.

"What are you doing?" The camera was aimed at me.

"Proving my point." The shutter clicked. He stood up and moved back a few feet, squinting at the low light in the room and fishing his light meter from the clutter on the table. Once he'd turned on a lamp on the desk behind him, he clicked off at least a dozen shots while I blushed and looked anywhere but at the lens.

"So shy," he teased in the husky voice that was the result of years of cigarettes, and probably what my grandmother would have called hard living. "Like you don't know exactly how pretty you are."

"Jackson." He had stopped being Mr. Devic the second day I'd worked for him, but that was months ago. Whatever we were now was much more than an employer and an employee, but less than lovers. "Cut it out. You're wasting film."

I held a hand up when he continued to shoot, ducking my head when he inched closer. As flirtations went, this was a new one, and it was uncomfortably exciting. He was so persistent, focused on me through the lens, and it was difficult not to think about what he found there that he liked—and what I might lack.

He was only shooting pictures of me, hardly out of character for a photographer, but something about his attention that night made my heart race. After a minute, I was blushing and sweating, and of course trying to hide it. My jeans felt too tight and my shirt felt too low cut. But as exciting as it was, it was also frightening, and that was ridiculous. Wasn't this what I'd planned on when I'd broken up with Michael? The freedom to choose, to figure out what I wanted, not to allow someone else, even someone I loved very much, to decide for me?

It wasn't as if Jackson hadn't flirted with me before. Just last week, we'd fallen asleep on the grungy old studio sofa together after sharing most of a bottle of wine, and I'd woken up to find my cheek against his chest and his arm flung over me. He was always rubbing my shoulders, touching my hair, bumping his hip against mine as we walked down the street. Every time he touched me, an electric tingle of awareness rippled through me like a promise. At least, it always had before.

But this time when he tipped my chin back to take a close-up of my face, I had to fight the urge to scramble out of my chair and run for the door. This time, I could see all the steps that would lead up to sleeping with him. If I decided to, I could make it happen, right now.

After a minute, he put down the camera and circled behind me. I was breathing so hard it was amazing I hadn't hyperventilated. Everything felt too big, too real, too loud, too close— I could feel Jackson's body heat behind me, hear the rasp of his boot soles on the gritty floor. When he rested his hands on my shoulders and bent to brush my hair away from the back of my neck, I was one huge exposed nerve, so sensitive I nearly groaned when his lips touched the vulnerable skin of my nape.

God, it felt good. After so long, after so many near misses, his mouth was teasing and sweet, but with just enough seriousness of purpose that it was clear he didn't intend to stop with one kiss. In fact, he was already moving on, trailing kisses up the side of my throat, twisting me in the chair until I was reaching for him without thinking twice. I stood up and he pulled me against him with rough, greedy hands, all wiry strength and hard edges.

And then I kissed him. He tasted of smoke

and beer and the spicy beef he'd eaten earlier, and the total effect was overwhelming—his mouth was a dark, strange place, his tongue hot and hungry and insistent, urging me on. Urging me closer, his hands in my hair and then on my back, fingering the belt loops of my jeans.

Swept away. The words flashed past in a blur, and I could feel it happening, the moment when it would be too late to stop was rushing toward me, and I knew then I couldn't go through with it.

It wasn't so much that I didn't love Jackson, or that he didn't love me. Suddenly, I understood the appeal of a strictly sexual relationship, a convenient way to scratch a certain itch and enjoy the hell out of it, too. But I could also see how easy it would be to go from Jackson to someone else, and someone else again, every kiss, every caress, taking me further from Michael.

That was when I knew that somewhere in the back of my mind, my separation from Michael had been temporary. A test, of sorts, for me as much as anyone. Maybe only for me. Loving Michael was a choice, it seemed, and very much mine.

I wriggled out of Jackson's arms, murmuring something trite and stupid, I'm sure—I don't remember the words now. What is there ever to say in that situation?

I remember all too well what he said, though. "It would have been good, Tess. It will be, whenever you're ready."

The thing was, I didn't doubt it. Jackson was sex on a stick—an older man with a lot of experience and the charm to make it seem desirable. But I knew when I left that night that "it" would never happen. I wasn't sure if I had ever really wanted it to, or if I had simply wanted the chance to say no.

I didn't quit right away. For two more weeks, we circled each other like restless cats, careful in what we said and when or how we touched, and I'd been foolish to think I could ignore what had passed between us and go back to being simply his employee. The day I left, he kissed me goodbye until I was literally weak in the knees, and crying. But I didn't blame him for rubbing my nose in what might have been, because it was all too clear by then that I wasn't a passing fancy for him, and that he didn't bed every young female assistant he hired. I was sorry to have hurt him, even if only his pride had been wounded.

The only thing that mattered to me then was how wounded Michael was. We hadn't talked in months, and I wanted nothing more than to call him that night, to hop on a bus to Boston and run straight to his apartment. But if I did that, I would have to mean it down to my bones. Better to wait, I thought. Give myself a little while, make sure I was deciding with my head as well as my heart.

If I hadn't waited, Drew Keating wouldn't have existed. Hindsight, as they say. And you know how that saying goes.

CHAPTER TEN

THE RAIN KEPT UP THROUGH MONDAY, effectively drowning any holiday-weekend spirit the three of us might have mustered. Emma wandered around the house aimlessly before taking off for her friend Nicole's house. The novelty of the weekend's drama had worn off, and she was back to pouting about the party she had missed, even though I would have chained her in her closet before letting her go, long-lost half brother or not. Michael had holed up at his desk, checking e-mail and searching for links to information about leukemia, and I retreated to the bedroom with Walter by noon, claiming laundry to fold. Instead, I curled up on the bed and stared out the window at the dripping leaves on the elm tree, with a huge mug of hot tea in one hand and Walter's head under the other.

My mother called twice—I had put off her questions when we picked up Walter Sunday night, but I still wasn't in any mood to discuss the situation yet, which I informed her much too curtly this morning. Nell had called, but that time I let the machine answer. She was still angry that I had missed the wedding planning, even if she wouldn't admit it, but I knew she was concerned about what Michael and I were going through, too.

Everyone was, of course. And everyone would likely switch directly into emergency mode when they learned that Drew was seriously ill. I couldn't help but love them for that, even though at the moment the idea of more questions and conversation made me want to draw the covers over my head for about a week.

Except that would leave me with nothing to do but face my own thoughts, and that was the last thing I wanted to do. Getting away from them today was hard enough. And as I finally turned to the pile of laundry on the bed and folded the towels into neat squares, I wondered if Michael was revisiting the past as he sat at his computer.

I had dreaded the moment he and Drew would walk into Sophia's apartment on Saturday. After twenty years, I had no idea how Michael and Sophia would greet each other. And there was something entirely too strange about the collection of people under that roof— a man with two children born of two different women, with both of the children and both of the women present?

In the end, I'm sure I was the only one buzzing with tension. Michael and Drew climbed the stairs, and when we walked into the hall to meet them, Michael and Sophia simply clasped hands for a moment before kissing each other lightly on the cheek.

But before Emma had broken down crying at the table, I'd noticed Michael exchanging glances with Sophia, sometimes even searching her face when she was busy talking to one of the kids. I couldn't blame him—*wouldn't* blame him—for having questions about Drew that only Sophia could answer. What his son's first word had been, maybe. If he had always loved drawing, what his favorite picture books were, when he'd kissed a girl for the first time.

What I didn't want to face was Michael revisiting the months he and Sophia had spent together. Remembering the reasons he'd fallen for her, slept with her. Appreciating the woman she was now.

It was jealousy, pure and simple, and I hated myself for it. After folding the last of the towels with something close to violence, I thrust them into the linen closet and slammed the door. Standing there in the upstairs hallway, my feet bare on the cool wood floor, I closed my eyes and took a deep breath.

It was stupid. Michael had come back to me, hadn't he? He'd spent the past twenty years with *me,* making a home, raising our daughter. Brushing my hair at night before we went to sleep, his fingers gentle as they stroked through the length of it. Calling me from work simply to tell me he missed me, or to share a silly story from the office. Making love to me in the bed we'd shared for so long, his mouth finding all my secret places, his weight and his whispered words so familiar, such a gift.

But that wasn't the whole story. Of course it wasn't. In those same twenty years we'd argued over everything from putting the trash out to the mortgage payment to the car breaking down. We'd let disagreements linger long past bedtime, hovering over us like a bad smell as we lay in bed, carefully not touching. He'd forgotten my birthday, or I'd forgotten his. We'd been too tired or too stressed to have sex, and then angry at each other for not initiating it.

Our life together wasn't perfect. No one's was, I was willing to bet. But not everyone had to watch her husband interact with a woman he'd once cared for a great deal, either.

"You okay up there?"

I jolted at the sound of Michael's voice drifting from the bottom of the stairs. He'd heard the door slam, then. Another proof of my childishness.

"I'm okay," I called back, and bit my lip. Another lie. "I stumbled into the door. Walter was underfoot." And now I was damning the dog by association. Perfect.

"You want some lunch?"

He sounded completely normal, at ease. And I knew him well enough to see through the casual question—he hoped I was hungry, too, so I would make lunch for both of us. Michael was wonderful about shoving a load of laundry in the washer or running the vacuum cleaner, but he was no cook.

So…that was normal. And normal was good. I called back, "I'll be right down."

But as we ate hastily thrown-together roast-beef sandwiches at the kitchen table, I watched his face anyway, for any sign that he was re-membering those long-ago days with Sophia. For the smallest proof that he was regretful, that he believed he had chosen wrong.

And I waited for him to talk to me, to ask me what I thought about Drew's illness or his chances. Instead, he paged through the morning paper, glancing up at me from time to time as he reached for another potato chip.

But he didn't ask why I was staring at him. He didn't ask what was on my mind, or how I felt about the events of the weekend. And that wasn't normal. Neither was the nearly guilty flash of confusion in his eyes when he folded the paper and retreated to his desk, leaving me alone with the dishes and a knot tightening in my throat.

I WAS GRATEFUL FOR THE RETURN to the daily routine on Tuesday. No More Wallowing. That was my motto as I got Michael off to the train and dug lunch money out of the bottom of my purse for Emma. I had work to do, of both the domestic and paying variety, and I fully intended to make a sweep through the house that morning before settling in with the photographs I'd taken so far for the book.

The sun had come out again, and the air was sweet and still damp from yesterday's rain. Walter collapsed in a circle of sunlight by the front door as I thrust open the windows and picked up junk mail and odds and ends in an old pair of jeans and a Joffrey Ballet T-shirt from three seasons ago. The plan was to dust, vacuum and possibly damp-mop the wood floors before lunchtime. A clean house always made me more settled, and each task was something I could plunge into with the stereo on to drown out my thoughts. Today called for loud and kick-ass, so I popped Springsteen's *Darkness on the Edge of Town* into the CD player.

I was singing along to "Badlands," dust rag in hand, when Walter sprang to his feet and sent out a joyful bark. The mailman, I assumed, although it was early—Walter's bark was always joyful. If a serial killer showed up, bloody knife in hand, Walter would greet him with a wagging tail and a "pet me" expression in his soulful doggy eyes.

"Anyone here?" The familiar voice came through the screen door, and I whirled to see Lucy standing on the other side of it. "Hello?"

"Lucy!" I threw the dust rag on the coffee table and darted over to the stereo to turn down the music, waving her in at the same time. "What are you doing here?"

She looked up from scratching behind Walter's ears with a saucy grin. Her ginger hair was pulled into a French twist, and a pair of sleek black sunglasses were perched on top of her head. In her neatly pressed khakis and white blouse, she could have stepped out of a glossy magazine ad for the Perfect Professional Woman.

"I was in the neighborhood," she said, striding across the hall to hug me. "And I haven't seen your face in way too long."

It was true—we relied on e-mail and infrequent phone calls to keep in touch now, with her in Baltimore working for the city planner. The last time we'd been in the same room was more than nine months ago.

"Well, I'm glad you're here," I told her, hugging her back for an extra minute. If she saw the tears in my eyes, I would be in trouble, but the sheer relief of seeing a friendly face—and one who had heard nothing about our family's strange news—was enough to make me dizzy. "Can you stay long?"

"Unfortunately, not really." She followed me into the kitchen, where I opened the fridge to search out bottles of iced tea. "I was here all weekend, but when I came around on Saturday, you weren't here. I swung by your mom's and she said you went to Cambridge."

She sat at the kitchen table, her bag and keys tossed casually on the surface. Even staring into the refrigerator I couldn't miss the question in her tone.

"We were back by Sunday evening," I said, and turned to hand her a Snapple. "How's *your* mom?"

She arched one well-groomed eyebrow. "Don't change the subject. What on earth were you doing in Cambridge? Did Michael have a college reunion or something?"

Lucy hadn't gotten to where she was by being a pushover. Hell, she hadn't been a pushover in high school. And I wasn't going to lie to her—she would have to know about Drew, too. So much for a good long girls' chat about nothing but fluff. Still, telling her the truth didn't mean I had to dive in headfirst.

"It was a family thing." I pulled out the chair opposite hers and sat down, then drew my knees up and wrapped my arms around them. "Do you want some lunch? What time is it, anyway?" I made a show of checking my watch, and she rolled her eyes.

"You're possibly the worst liar in the world, you know that?" She leaned across the table to narrow her eyes at me. "Michael doesn't have family in Cambridge and neither do you."

A half laugh escaped. "He does now."

She dragged the whole story out of me then, punctuating everything I told her with a question or a curse or shocked amazement. I revealed it all, even my reasons for separating from Michael. By the time I was done, she had slumped back in her chair, listening as she focused on the slowly circling fan on the ceiling.

"So Michael's going up later this week to take some tests to determine if he's a bone marrow match," I finished. I carefully omitted the chance, another elephant living in the room with Michael and me, that Emma might need to do the same thing. "After that, well, it will depend on the results."

She sat up and leveled her gaze at me as I cracked open my bottle of iced tea. "And you're okay with all of this?"

"Okay with Michael helping to save Drew's life if that's possible? Of course I am."

"Not with *that*." Lucy scraped her chair away from the table and stood up to pace the length of the kitchen. "With everything else! Jesus, Tess, what's wrong with you? You find out Michael slept with another woman, and you're completely calm about it? And what the hell is this Sophia's problem? How selfish is that, to give birth to this kid and never tell the child's father? And then when he *needs* something, it's a different story."

Her outrage was so unexpected, so violent in the sunny, quiet kitchen, it was like a spark, lighting my own fury. What on earth did she have to be so angry about?

I put my iced tea down on the old maple table with a resounding *thunk*. "Did you ever stop to think that I'm grateful for what you claim is Sophia's selfishness? If she'd told Michael she was pregnant all those years ago, what would have happened then? What would my life be right now?"

"That's not the point." Lucy was dug in already, I could tell, prepared to argue her point until I capitulated. She leaned against the counter and folded her arms over her chest. "The point is—"

"The point is that this is my life, Lucy! Mine and Michael's, and Emma's, too. And no matter what you think about it, it's shaken every one of us down to our bones. And it did *before* we knew Drew was ill." I bit my bottom lip. Tears were threatening already, hot and urgent, and I choked out the words past the lump in my throat. "God, Lucy, I would have expected at least a little sympathy. Support would be even better, all right?"

"Tess, you don't get it!" She crossed the room to lean over me, and rested her head against mine as she wound an arm around my shoulders. "I do support you, honey. So much. I'm just…I'm just appalled that Michael did this. I'm having a hard time believing it."

I shrugged away from her and stood, wiping the tears away with the back of my hand like a child. "But I told you, it's not his fault. *I* broke up with *him,* Lucy. I broke up with him because I wanted to sleep with someone else. Was

Michael supposed to intuit that I would want to get back together?"

Her sharp, sepia eyes still held fury—she wasn't giving in, not yet. "I don't know. But it doesn't change that he did this and never told you about it. And that she kept it from him— that's unforgivable, if you ask me. If this poor kid hadn't gotten sick, Michael still wouldn't know he had a son!"

I shook my head and sank to the floor, wrapping my arms around my knees again. "You're not making sense. You're mad that he slept with another woman, but you're also angry that he didn't get to know his son until now? Pick a side, Lucy."

"I'm on your side!" She crouched on the floor beside me, heedless of her pristine khakis and the grit I hadn't yet mopped. "God, of course I'm on your side! I don't know what side you're on, to be honest. I can't figure out why *you're* not furious and upset."

"You think I'm not upset? Are you kidding?" I laughed again, hating the bitter sound of it in the silence. "I spent the weekend meeting my husband's former lover and their son. We all had dinner together, in her apartment, for God's sake. Now my husband is trying to figure out how he can help save this boy's life. And I'm not upset?"

She sighed and sat down so we were shoulder to shoulder. Walter wandered in and flopped at our feet, panting up at us with hope in his eyes.

"I guess I'm surprised that you're not more upset with Michael and with this woman. They lied to you, to each other, to this kid…" She trailed off for a moment, absently stroking Walter's head when he wriggled up to meet her hand. "I would be furious at him if I were you. I am furious at him, and he's not even my husband. It's just that what you two have, what you've always had, is really special. I can't believe that there were secrets between you. That this Sophia person kept this secret for so long and decided to spring it now. It's just…it's weird."

Weird. There was an understatement.

And she still didn't get it. She didn't understand that I *was* broken by Michael's affair with Sophia, but was certain I had no right to be. That I was scared Michael had never trusted my love for him, that he didn't know even now I'd made a huge mistake letting him go.

Lucy couldn't possibly understand that I felt selfish and small because I had blithely assumed all these years that Michael had never betrayed me. That he would figure out I had taken his love for granted when I'd held my own back. And I couldn't explain it, couldn't say the words. Not now. Not yet. Not to her. Not to another person who held onto the idea that Michael and I were some mythic golden couple.

As if true love was easy or convenient. As if it would never raise a question or a doubt. What would it be worth if there was no struggle for it?

We limped through lunch after that, pretending to catch up on gossip and all the small, ordinary things that made up so much of our lives—Lucy's crazy boss, Emma's infatuation with this Jesse boy, my tentative plans to repaint my office, Lucy's latest blind date. But the words all sounded hollow, and Lucy had barely eaten her last bite of the tuna salad I'd thrown together when she kissed me goodbye and left.

I stood at the screen door and waved as she ran down the front walk to her little silver Camry, relieved that she had decided to leave so soon. But if I was glad to watch her go, why did I feel more alone than ever?

CHAPTER ELEVEN

BACK-TO-BACK PORTRAIT appointments kept me busy on Wednesday, which was a good thing. Wrangling a suspicious toddler into photo-worthy smiles wasn't easy, and it certainly didn't leave me any time to brood. The second appointment was a family shot—a couple and their four-year-old triplets—and it wasn't any easier, despite the parents' presence. By the time I pulled in to the driveway at home and parked the car, I was exhausted.

Being exhausted was beginning to seem like a permanent state of being. I'd left the house half-cleaned the day before, and the vacuum was still standing in the living room, a pointed reminder of all the tasks I'd been too tired or too dispirited to finish. Unfortunately, I couldn't simply walk away when it came to dealing with my daughter.

Emma teetered between genuine concern about Drew and giddy, completely selfish impatience about the prom Friday night. My mother had agreed to make a dress for her, but I hadn't yet agreed to let Emma stay out past midnight, despite her best efforts at lobbying for 1:00 a.m.

"We'll be in town, Mom," she said Wednesday afternoon when she arrived home from school. She'd tossed her backpack on the floor in the front hall and now sat on the sofa, where I had planted myself when I got home. "And we'll all be together, a big group. And I'll be home right at one, on the dot. Cross my heart—"

I glared up at her from the mail I had begun to sort, and she caught herself before she added "hope to die." I might have lost my sense of humor for the moment, but at least I had good reason.

"Mom, come on." With her hair loose around her face and her eyes wide and pleading, she might have been six again, asking for another Barbie or another book at bedtime. "Everyone else is staying out till one. And I missed the party last weekend—"

I held up a hand to cut her off and threw the unread mail on the coffee table. "Emma, you have to understand something. Whether or not we went to Cambridge, you were never going to a party down the shore." I waited until her gaze flicked up to mine, hot with resentment now, and lowered the final boom. "*Never.*"

"God, Mom!" She stood up, practically quivering with outrage. "You just don't get it! This is my life, and you're ruining it!"

If I hadn't been so overwhelmed and stressed already, I might have been tempted to laugh. As it was, I felt like recording the words in her baby book—"The first time Emma accused me of ruining her life." Just like a toddler's first word, this was only the beginning, and I knew it.

But I wasn't backing down. Emma was all over the place, upset and worried about Drew one minute, resentful and angry at Michael and me the next, then swooning over Jesse and/or crowing about the play, which was in final rehearsals. At least half of the mood swings could be chalked up to teenage hormones running amok, but the other half were a direct result of the news about Drew. I wasn't sure she could be trusted to brush her teeth right now, much less stay out far too late with an older boy.

"I know it's your life, Em." I stood up, too, but she saw me coming and wrenched herself out of reach before I could put my arm around her. "But part of life is learning that there are limits to what you can do. And it's up to me and Daddy to help set those limits. You can stay out till midnight, but no later. And if you're not happy with that, you can stay home."

She was trying hard not to cry, and my heart squeezed in sympathy before she lobbed her parting shot. "Oh, don't worry, Cinderella's going to the ball."

A long time ago I had been exactly where she was, a tangled mess of confusion and yearning and fledgling independence. Every teenage girl has been. But there was no way to explain that to her. At that age, you can't hear it, and there's no way to accept it. At fifteen your pain is bigger than anything in the world and much more important.

"Nana is coming by tomorrow with your dress," I offered as she snatched up her backpack and ran up the stairs. I didn't know if she'd heard me as she clattered up the steps to her room, but I wasn't going after her. Not now. There was only so much angst I could take in one afternoon, and Michael and I were making enough of our own.

He'd retreated into his head since we'd returned from Massachusetts. Every day he went a little deeper, a little further away from me. I knew all too well how many things had to be fighting for space in his mind—memories, fears, hope, confusion—but so far he wasn't willing to share them, or to let me shoulder the burden for a little while. We were again behaving like strangers, silently passing each other on the way to the bathroom or as we loaded the dishwasher, barely touching in bed at night.

I was so lonely I could have screamed. The space Michael had always taken up was hollow for now, a chilly blankness where there had always been the warmth of his touch, his scent, spicy and male, the familiar sound of his voice, the sheer comfort of knowing he was there, present, *with* me. And the worst of it was that he was leaving tomorrow to fly back to Cambridge for the tests that would determine if he was a bone marrow match. He'd be gone until Saturday evening, too.

I sighed and glanced back down at the mail. Bills mostly, and I didn't have the heart to even look at them at the moment. I left the tumbled pile where it lay and ignored the day's accumulated mess to climb the stairs myself. Michael wouldn't be home for hours, and I had the film from the day's shoots to sort through and label until I had a chance to develop it. There were a million other tasks I'd neglected—curling up on the bed to cry wasn't an option. Emma was probably doing it for me, anyway.

But when I stopped at her door, expecting

to hear muffled sobs, if not her stereo blasting, I was surprised to be met with silence. No, wait, not silence—she was talking to someone on the phone.

Jesse. She said his name, and followed it with a little laugh. It was a wistful sound, and I heard the evidence of recent tears in her husky voice, but the point was that this boy had coaxed her out of her mood. This boy I knew next to nothing about. A boy I assumed she had called before Grace or Nicole, her stalwarts.

One step at a time, I reminded myself, and tiptoed away from the door into my office, as guilty as a thief. She was going to the dance with Jesse on Friday, after all. Logic demanded that they speak to each other once in a while.

But "one step at a time" meant so many things. It was a reminder to myself to deal with the biggest issues first. To wait for Michael to be tested before I freaked out about what donating bone marrow would mean.

And right now it looked as though Jesse was taking steps to becoming Emma's boyfriend. A few flirtations in the cafeteria, a phone call or two, an invitation to a dance. Nothing out of the ordinary there.

The steps Emma was preparing to take were what really worried me.

WHEN MICHAEL LEFT FOR Boston his freshman year, I was positive that my heart had been cut out. Those first few days without him were torture—I was right back to where I had been when the summer started. I daydreamed about being in bed with the blinds closed, staring at the ceiling, grieving, crying, sleeping to escape.

Even seventeen-year-olds can be extremely melodramatic.

We hadn't courted, if such an old-fashioned term was applied then. We hadn't gotten to know each other, not in the slow, tentative way some couples do, over time. We'd devoured each other in just under a week, talking until our throats were dry, our bodies always touching, even if it was only our hands, or our ankles hooked one over the other as we pushed the creaky old swing on my porch into motion. We memorized each other, swallowing each other up in our eagerness, and by the time we slept together, I couldn't remember what life had been like before Michael's kisses, his comfortable weight on top of me or his shuddering body beneath me.

Our plan had been for me to ride up to Cambridge with him and his mother, of course. We wanted every minute we could have together, even if it was chaperoned by a parent and a little sister. But before Mrs. Butterfield could weigh in, my mother vetoed the idea.

"Absolutely not," she said, and she didn't even glance up from the hem she was finishing on the sewing machine. I'd found her, as usual, in the dining room, fabrics and trims mounded on the table beside her sewing machine. "Maureen will have her hands full enough between the drive and getting Michael settled in. She certainly doesn't need you along—"

She stopped short, something else on the tip of her tongue. Something unflattering, I was sure. Something about me weeping or being a drama queen—she'd blown up at me just the day before because I burst into tears at the dinner table when Will teased me about how many pretty Radcliffe girls Michael was bound to meet.

"I can help," I argued. It was difficult not to fidget, to keep still, when I wanted to plead and scream. "I can keep Melissa busy in the car and the hotel room, and I can help carry things up to the dorm…"

Mom didn't bother to say no again. She simply turned that resolute, impatient glare on me, a threaded needle clenched between her teeth, until I gave up and walked away. Well, stomped away. There was no sense in presenting the calm adult facade when she'd said no.

"There's always Lucy's car," Cath said a month later. We were sprawled on the living-room floor at my house, with *General Hospital* on in the background and a litter of empty diet soda cans and Pringles crumbs on the coffee table. She was tackling AP calculus, while I pretended to study French vocabulary. A letter from Michael had come in the mail, and I had spent the past twenty minutes alternating between reading bits of it aloud to her and moaning about how long it would be before I saw him again.

"What does Lucy's car have to do with anything?"

Cath arched her pierced eyebrow at me. A delicate silver hoop was in place today. "It's transportation, you idiot. As in, it could *transport* you to Harvard."

"Like my mother would ever let Lucy and me drive up to Boston," I snorted, and flopped over on my back on the carpet.

"She doesn't have to know." Cath tossed her notebook on the table and leaned over. "Think about it. You could tell her you're sleeping over at her house, and then the next night you call and say we're all sleeping at my place. Meanwhile, you're in Michael's dorm room."

Round robin. A time-honored tradition, but

one with risks. Especially when I wouldn't be just across town at a party, but four states away.

"And where would you and Lucy be?" I sat up, frowning, and tried to figure out how the plan could work. "In the dorm room with us?"

"You need a remedial class in evil plotting, immediately." She sighed. "We'd be here at home, dummy. You'd take Lucy's car."

"And you think Lucy would let me do that why exactly…?"

That stopped her cold. She reached into the tall red tube and withdrew another Pringles, then bit into it thoughtfully. "I could twist her arm. You'd have to practice with the VW, though. You suck at stick shift."

"Thanks," I said, and hugged my knees tightly to my chest. Excitement had rippled through me like a gust of wind—if I didn't hold on, it would blow me away.

I could do it, I thought. Sure, I did kind of suck at driving a stick shift, but I could practice. How hard could it be, really? And if it meant being with Michael for a whole weekend—before Thanksgiving, which would involve way too much family time, way too much food and nowhere near enough opportunities to touch each other— I'd learn how to fly, if that was what it took.

"This could work," I said, and grinned at

Cath, who nodded at me as if I were a six-year-old finally grasping a concept as simple as one plus one. "I've got money saved, I can pay for gas, I can drive up there on a Friday afternoon and then—"

"Drive *where?*"

Shit. My mother stood in the arch between the living room and the front hall, an overflowing basket of laundry in her arms and her eyes blazing fire.

"Um…" Hadn't she been upstairs?

"Cath, you'll be going home now," Mom said evenly, and Cath didn't hesitate. She scooped her books into her bag and managed only a brief sympathetic glance at me before she was out the front door, her combat boots thudding down the steps.

Showdown time. Just me and the immovable force that my mother had become—at least, when Michael was involved. "Mom, I don't know what you heard, but I can—"

"I don't have to hear anything else, Tess." She set down the laundry basket and balanced on the edge of the coffee table, nudging my homework out of the way, elbows on her knees. Her jeans were just as faded as mine, and her hair was knotted messily on top of her head. In her plain white button-down shirt, she looked young, I thought, so much younger than other moms. But even as I had the thought, I noticed the lines around her eyes, the shadow of anxiety beneath them. For the first time her eyes looked old.

"I know you miss him, Tess. I know you…love him, and believe me, I think Michael is a wonderful boy. Really, I do. But I'm worried, honey. You're eating, breathing and sleeping nothing but him. You're talking about taking off in a car by yourself and driving hours away when he'll be here for Thanksgiving in just a matter of weeks. I don't want to restrict you to the house, but there's no way you're driving up to Harvard, I can tell you that right now."

Amazing how excitement could flare into hot, smoldering ash so quickly. "You didn't seem to care when dancing was all I thought about."

She groaned and shook her head. "Yeah, well, I'm scared that's part of the problem. Ballet was a passion for you, baby. A *calling*. Let's face it, if it wasn't for your knee, you'd still be dancing. So what scares me is that you simply replaced one love with another."

I felt as if she'd slapped me. I loved Michael because of who he was, not because he was convenient. He was so much more than that to me. He *was*.

I couldn't answer her—tears were stinging my

eyes, escaping even as I fled up the stairs to my room. In that moment, I hated her. Flopped on my bed, my flushed cheek against the pillowcase and the window wrenched open to let in the early-October chill, I cried until there was nothing left.

And I hated myself when I was done. Maybe my mother was the first person to suggest out loud that Michael was nothing more than a distraction while I figured out what the hell my life would become now that ballet wasn't a part of it. But she wasn't the first person to suspect it. If I was going to be completely honest with myself, I couldn't deny that sometimes I was scared of the same thing.

EMMA REFUSED TO COME down for dinner, claiming she didn't feel well. I didn't have the energy to argue with her, and Michael blew off her rebellion. "She's entitled to a few tantrums right now," he said, sitting down across from me.

"You really believe that?" I set his plate down a little too hard, and a cherry tomato rolled onto the place mat.

He stared at me as he picked up the tomato and popped it into his mouth. "Yeah, I do. She's had some pretty major news the past few weeks, none of it what you could call good."

"Do you think I don't know that, Michael?" I dished some of the pasta primavera onto my plate and grabbed my glass of iced tea before I sat down. "Somehow that's not keeping her from obsessing about this kid Jesse, or the dance or how late she can stay out Friday night."

"I don't know what you want me to say, Tess." He dropped his fork and pinched the bridge of his nose between his thumb and forefinger, a giveaway that he had a headache. "Do you want to ground her for being angry at you? Do you want her to completely lose it, or would you rather she was at least still doing all the things normal teenage girls do?" He raised those dark, wounded eyes to mine, and for the first time I swore I saw accusations in them. Did he think I was overreacting? Did he even care how I felt about all of this? Did he understand how terrified I was that this would pull us apart, irrevocably?

The silence hummed between us, broken only by a dog barking somewhere in the neighborhood. I pushed my plate away and got up, and managed to make it to the bedroom before the tears fell. I was asleep when he came to bed hours later, and when I got up in the morning, he had already left for the airport.

It was the first time we had ever parted

without saying goodbye. It was the only time since we'd been married that we had parted without saying *I love you.*

CHAPTER TWELVE

"ISN'T SHE BEAUTIFUL," MY MOTHER said Thursday afternoon, sitting amid the rumpled covers on Emma's bed.

Emma twirled in front of the mirror fixed to her closet door. "It's awesome, Nana. No one else will have a dress like this."

It was gorgeous, not that I'd expected anything else. My mother hadn't made a name for herself designing clothes for nothing. It was elegant without being too mature, it was form-fitting enough to show off Emma's budding curves without being obscene and, of course, it looked as if it had been made for her. A deep creamy satin with a square neckline and one-inch straps, the dress had a skirt that was two layers, with a film of embroidered cream tulle on top—embroidery Mom had mimicked in beaded detail on the bodice. I had been worried the dress would be too pale against Emma's fair skin and blond hair, but Mom had covered that.

She'd beaded the delicate leaves on the bodice in black and echoed them on the hem of the satin skirt. With black heels and a pair of black pearl earrings Mom had loaned for the occasion, Emma was radiant. I knew just which red lipstick I would give her to wear Friday night.

"It's lovely," I said, and smiled into the mirror at Emma, who was still admiring herself. I nudged my mother's arm playfully. "You should do this for a living, you know?"

"There's a thought." But she was pleased with herself, and scooted backward on the bed to lean against the pillows. "Quite a race, though. I haven't beaded that fast in years. Next time a little more notice would be nice, please."

"Done." I sat down beside her and fought back a sudden lump in my throat when Mom wound her arm around my shoulders and stroked my hair. No matter how old I got, it would always be tempting to let her hug away my problems.

"You okay?" she murmured. "Did Michael get to Boston all right?"

I nodded, answering the second question if not the first. Michael had called when he landed at Logan, and we'd apologized to each other by the time we said our goodbyes. Even so, the conversation was stiff, a little forced, and I was relieved when we hung up. It was an awful feeling.

"I should wear this every day," Emma said with a sigh. "Every*where*. It's, like, the most perfect dress ever." She turned one more time, the skirt flaring just enough to qualify as "twirly" without appearing as if it had been made for a ballroom dancer. "Can I borrow your little black bag, Mom?"

"Absolutely." I held up a finger. "If you let me take pictures before you leave."

"As if I have a choice," she groaned. "Unzip me?"

I stood up to help her out of the dress, and Mom followed, kissing Emma's cheek before she said, "I'll make some tea. I think I deserve a cookie for my efforts. Or possibly cake."

"I'll be down in a minute," I said, and Emma called out her thanks for approximately the fourteenth time. When the dress was properly on its hanger and in her closet, I took her chin in my fingers and leaned in close. "You are beautiful, sweetheart. And entirely too grown-up."

"*Mom.*" But she was grinning when I closed the bedroom door behind me.

"I found your secret stash," Mom said as I walked into the kitchen, and held up a box of Girl Scout cookies.

"They're Emma's," I said primly, and shook

tea bags out of the box since the kettle was about to whistle.

We let the quiet envelop us for a minute as I poured the boiling water into a teapot. Walter was dozing at Mom's feet. Already, drowsy carpenter bees buzzed in the wisteria climbing the trellis, and somewhere outside little girls were chanting the familiar words to "Ring Around the Rosy."

As I reached for mugs, Mom spoke up. "I wish you would talk to me, honey. I feel so helpless. And you look, well, awful."

She surprised a laugh out of me. "Thanks, Mom."

"Well, it's true," she protested. She frowned as I carried the mugs of tea to the table, her brow furrowed in concern. "You look like you haven't slept in weeks. And you must be apprehensive about what Michael's going through up there."

I'd finally told her about the weekend in Cambridge, meeting Drew, and Sophia, face-to-face, and of course Drew's illness. I'd told her why Michael was in Massachusetts, and while she approved of his efforts to help, it didn't worry her any less that it was the right thing to do.

"I'm not apprehensive." I blew on my tea, sending steam curling away toward the ceiling. "The initial test is easy—apparently it's just a swab in his cheek. The results of that will determine whether they do more specific testing. And even that won't cause anything more than a little discomfort."

"That's not what I meant, and you know it."

I played dumb, which was childish, but I wasn't about to spill my guts, not when Michael and I hadn't even talked about half the things on my mind. "No, I don't. What did you mean, Mom?"

I might have been six years old again, squirming as she stared at me, eyebrows raised as she patiently waited for me to admit that I'd spilled the orange juice or broken the dish.

"Maybe *apprehensive* was the wrong word," she said finally. Her clipped tone made it clear she wasn't pleased with my lie. "Maybe I should have used *angry* or *resentful* instead."

I sighed, and glanced out the back door. In my head, I could see Michael knocking on Sophia's door, his overnight bag slung over one shoulder, his hair mussed the way it always was when he was restless, the three of them sitting down to dinner in that bright little kitchen…

Shutting my eyes to erase the image, I met Mom's gaze again. "I can't be resentful that he's helping to save his son's life, can I? Who would be angry about that?"

"No one, honey. But if I were you, I would

be goddamn pissed off that he had to do it at all. That he had to be away the night of his daughter's first prom." She stopped and took a deep breath, gathering her thoughts and leaning forward to lay her hand over mine. "I love Michael very much, and I understand that you two were…apart when Drew was conceived, but that can't make the consequences any easier to deal with. If you're mad, you need to let it out. Cry, scream. Just get rid of all the worry, even for a minute. You're walking around like a ticking time bomb, and if you think the people who love you can't see in your eyes how much you hurt, you're wrong."

So much for not crying. A stray tear dropped into the mug I was still holding to my mouth, and I watched as it rippled into a widening circle. I'd made a choice twenty years ago, a difficult, completely personal choice I never imagined would affect anyone but Michael and me. Instead, suddenly everyone I loved was involved in some way—and a boy who might not have existed otherwise possibly wouldn't survive the year.

I managed to put my mug down before I spilled it, and let Mom hold me while I sobbed.

I ANSWERED THE DOOR WHEN Jesse knocked Friday night. A classic black limo was idling at the curb, which surprised me. He was a year older than Emma, probably at the far end of sixteen, too, but I had expected one of his parents to drive them to the dance. The idea that he didn't have his license yet had seemed like a good thing yesterday. Imagining my daughter and this very charming boy in the big back seat of a limo was a whole other story.

"Hi, Mrs. Butterfield," he said as I pushed open the screen door to let him in. "I'm Jesse."

"We met once," I reminded him, and suddenly wanted to smack myself for not insisting that Emma have him over before tonight. I was supposed to be vigilant about this stuff, and here I was letting her go off with a boy I didn't know at all, even if it was only to the high-school gym across town.

He was truly a golden boy, I decided as he sat down on the living-room sofa, more comfortable than I would have guessed for a kid his age. Blond and already tanned, with huge brown eyes and shiny white teeth thanks to some genius orthodontist, he was tall and leanly muscled, the standard dreamboat. I hated him, in his classic black tux and shiny confidence, just a little.

"I'll go get Emma," I said, furious that Michael wasn't there to grill him with some clichéd fatherly questions. That he wasn't there to see his daughter off to her first big dance with a hug. Before Jesse could reply, I fled up the stairs.

Emma was ready when I knocked on her door, zipped into her dress, wearing my mother's earrings and her own black heels, warm red lipstick on her mouth. She whirled once, already giddy with excitement, and struck a showroom model's pose.

"How do I look?" The pink in her cheeks wasn't entirely due to cosmetics. And the contrast of my daughter in her very grown-up dress against the happy lilac walls of her room and the bedspread with its pop-art daisies was a jarring one.

"You look beautiful," I said. It was true. It was also somehow heartbreaking. At that moment I could envision her as a young woman of twenty, twenty-five, thirty, and I longed to snatch her up in my arms and hold her until this boy gave in and went away. "Jesse's waiting downstairs."

"I know." Her eyes widened. "I saw the limo. Cool, huh?"

I made an agreeable noise to keep from saying anything unpleasant and checked on the mess of her bed for the black evening purse.

"You have some money? Do you need anything else? The red lipstick? Gum?"

"I'm good, Mom." She surprised me with a kiss, her lips brushing my cheek in a fleeting gesture of gratitude. "Let's go get the pictures over with, huh?"

Jesse was waiting in the hall when we came down the stairs, and the dazzle in his eyes when he caught sight of Emma was gratifying. And worrying, to be honest—for a moment I was convinced he would swallow her whole. But he held out the single red rose corsage like a gentleman, and I helped Emma pin it to the strap of her dress before positioning them for a picture.

"Okay, you two," I said when it was clear Emma was restless with posing. "Have fun. I'll expect you at midnight."

She managed an "uh-huh" before escaping through the door, where Jesse took her hand to lead her down to the limo. I followed them onto the porch in my bare feet, the camera still clutched in one hand as I debated whether to yell out a reminder about the curfew. It was a humiliating prospect for both Emma and me, and while I was still arguing with myself, they climbed into the car, the door shutting behind them with a *thunk*. I'd have to trust her—it wasn't as if we hadn't argued the point endlessly all week.

And then they were gone, and Walter and I were alone in the house, a rarity on a Friday evening. Michael almost never traveled, and I couldn't remember the last time he'd been away on a weekend. As Friday nights were traditionally our at-home night, when we were both too exhausted by the week's grind to cook or go out—Saturday nights were for restaurants or the occasional movie or party with friends. Fridays were for us, for decadent take-out food and a rented movie popped into the DVD player as we settled into each other on the sofa, idly discussing the week or the weekend to come. It was for going to bed early, as long as Emma wasn't out babysitting, and learning each other all over again in the quiet dark of our bedroom.

I had plenty to do to keep me busy until Emma got home, of course. The checkbook was due to be balanced, I had film to develop, and there was always laundry piled somewhere. I didn't have to let the hollow silence in the house echo in my head. I would make myself busy—and I would start with junk food.

One gooey, cheesy pizza and two loads of laundry later and I was still at loose ends. If only the phone would ring or my sister would stop by unexpectedly. What I didn't want was to closet myself in the darkroom downstairs with only my thoughts for company.

I tidied the living and dining rooms, picking up all the odds and ends that had accumulated over the past few days. I took the upstairs things upstairs and put one of Emma's books and a CD in her room. The light cotton lap quilt I'd grabbed from the sofa usually lived in the guest room—Michael had brought it downstairs on Monday, when the incessant rain had made the evening chilly.

We were lucky to have a proper guest room, not that it was used very often. With only one child, though, space wasn't at quite the premium it was in some of my friends' houses. I had the small fourth bedroom as my office, and Michael had turned a tiny room off the kitchen into his—both of us liked the cozy confines, and having little space for anything but a desk and a computer cut down on distractions. So the guest room stood empty most of the time, partly extra storage for things, partly home to our oldest furniture.

I folded the quilt and put in on the end of the bed, then sat down. Lucy had been our last guest, on New Year's Eve. I couldn't imagine when the room would be used next, and then it hit me with a jolt—Drew. Drew might like to visit his father, possibly Emma and me, and he would stay here. I glanced around the room in the twilight, and although the gloom softened the rough edges of the mismatched furniture and the few plastic bins of winter clothes that had never made it up to the attic, the unfinished neglect of the room was depressing. There was a project, if I needed one. I could paint, buy a new comforter and some new curtains, frame a couple of pictures for the walls, refinish the dresser Michael had used when he was a kid.

The idea of undertaking the task was overwhelming. The idea of Drew staying with us was simply surreal. Slightly sick to my stomach, which had to be the result of too much pizza, I wandered back downstairs and curled into the sofa with the remote control. It was only eight-thirty—a few hours of nonsense on television wouldn't hurt.

I flipped channels with Walter snoring beside me, and finally settled on an Audrey Hepburn movie on PBS—*Roman Holiday,* I decided. Yes, there they were at the Mouth of Truth. I put down the remote and lay back.

When Walter pawed at my thigh, his nails too long for comfort, I glanced up to find a documentary about the Grateful Dead on the screen. Shit—I had dozed off. The house was dark but for the single lamp burning on the end table beside me. Scrambling upright, I looked at my watch. It was nearly one-thirty in the morning.

Poor Walter, I thought, realizing he hadn't been out, and then gasped. *Emma*. Where the hell was Emma?

She could have come home and decided not to wake me, I reasoned as I bounded up the stairs, still a little dizzy with sleep, my heart stuttering. She could have. It was possible.

But not true, of course. The door to her bedroom stood open to the dark hall, and when I flipped the light switch inside the room, her bed was empty, the same mass of tangled covers and discarded clothes it had been when she'd left.

"Oh my God." I swallowed hard, only vaguely aware of Walter beside me, tail thumping in concern, his doggy breath moist against my calf. *"Oh my God."*

I couldn't panic. I *wouldn't* panic. I would very calmly… Do what? As I stood frozen in the dark upstairs hallway, my mind raced. Who was I supposed to call? Jesse's parents? The limo company? I didn't know which one Jesse had used.

Emma's cell phone. Right. She had a phone just for emergencies, and this definitely qualified.

"Of course she could have used it to call me,"

I muttered, running back downstairs to the phone in the kitchen and the list of numbers posted on the fridge.

My hands shook with the rush of adrenaline as I fumbled the phone off the base and dialed Emma's cell. But even doing that didn't stop my imagination from producing scenarios. An accident in the limo. Emma and Jesse in the back seat of the limo, parked somewhere. The limo speeding down the parkway to the shore.

Her phone rang and rang until voice mail picked up: "This is Emma. I'll call you back!"

I hung up without bothering to leave a message. If she could hear her phone and wasn't picking up because she saw it was me, she wouldn't check her voice mail. And if she couldn't hear her phone, well…I didn't want to know what that meant.

The clock ticking above the kitchen table read 1:45. An hour and forty-five minutes past her curfew. Defiance? Forgetfulness? A boy who looked charming but had slipped a rufie into her fruit punch?

"Oh God," I said again, startling Walter. I had to find her. If only to kill her with my bare hands later. I scrambled into the front hall, grabbing a pair of sneakers and jammed my bare feet into them. I was reaching for the car keys I had tossed on the table sometime earlier, when I realized I couldn't leave. Michael wasn't here— if I went out to search for Emma, what would happen if she came home? What would happen if the police showed up?

Just the idea of that was ice in my blood. I swallowed back a panicked sob. *Stay calm,* I told myself firmly. *Stop it.*

I looked at my watch: 1:48. Well, this was what sisters were for, wasn't it?

And their fiancés, I thought when Jack answered the phone and croaked out, "Hello?"

"Jack, it's Tess." From somewhere far away, I realized my voice wasn't trembling. That was good. I was calm. I had to stay that way, even if I was beginning to tremble. "Can you and Nell help me? Emma hasn't come home."

CHAPTER THIRTEEN

"WHAT THE HELL WERE you thinking?"

Even I flinched at the vicious bite in Michael's voice. I had never heard him so furious with Emma.

I'd dragged Emma with me to pick him up at the airport this morning. After her stunt the night before, I wasn't letting her out of my sight until she was thirty. Michael had only heard the thumbnail version on the phone, and he'd chosen to wait until we got home to have it out with her and get the details.

She was slumped on the sofa, her pose, her face oozing defiance. My fingers nearly itched with the need to jerk her upright and tell her to pay attention, but I was almost afraid to move. It felt too much like everything was falling apart—if I didn't watch myself, I would shatter into pieces, wounding Emma and Michael when I broke.

"I wasn't 'thinking' anything," she said

sullenly, and crossed her arms over her chest. In her old Buffy the Vampire Slayer T-shirt and faded shorts, she wasn't anything at all like the young woman who had walked out of the house last night. This morning she was a child through and through, down to her scruffy ponytail and her pout. "I was just having fun."

"Oh, well, all's forgiven, then." Michael heaved a sigh rich with exasperation and dropped into the chair opposite her, raking a hand through his hair restlessly. "What exactly happened last night?"

Where to begin? The distance between saying goodbye to Emma yesterday evening and right now felt like years.

Jack and Nell had arrived right away, Nell in a pair of striped pajama bottoms and a stained white T-shirt, her eyes still foggy with sleep. She would wait at home while Jack and I took separate cars and circled through town—both of us knew well enough how to spot a party. In the meantime, Nell would call one of her friends in the E.R. at the hospital. "Just in case," she said as I headed out to my car, but her eyes were dark with worry.

In the end it was Jack who found her, and called me on my cell phone from outside a huge old house way down on Lawrence

Avenue, where he had a humiliated and angry Emma already bundled into his car. I pulled into a parking spot on Broad Street for just a second, burst into noisy, relieved tears, then drove home to meet them, my hands shaking the whole way.

"A party?"

For a minute, I was actually afraid Michael would launch out of his chair and throttle her— he radiated a blaze already nearly out of control.

"We just thought we'd go for a little while," Emma insisted. She'd begun to cry. The tears made jagged silver rivers on her cheeks. "We lost track of time, that's all."

Exactly what she'd told me last night, outraged and sobbing in the kitchen, where Nell had made tea and Jack stood by the back door, as uncomfortable as I'd ever seen him.

"And what time did you leave the dance?"

Here was the problem, I thought, rubbing my eyes as I perched on the arm of the sofa. I hadn't gotten her to admit anything more than the vague "before midnight," even after Nell and Jack had left. And it didn't really matter in the end—what mattered was that she hadn't made curfew, hadn't even attempted to make curfew, and hadn't bothered to call and at least let me know she was all right. If Emma believed her

father was going to let her get by on a techni-
cality, she was as wrong as a three-dollar bill.

"I don't remember. Everyone was going to
Billy Needham's, and we all kind of left
together." She sniffled and wiped at her wet
cheeks with the back of one hand.

"Aside from the fact that you had no business
going anywhere after the dance, let me ask you
this." Michael leaned forward, his jaw set tight.
"Were Mr. and Mrs. Needham home?"

She swallowed hard and stared into her lap.
"Um, no."

"And are you allowed to go to parties when
there are no parents present?"

Instead of answering, she was crying in
earnest, the huge, gulping sobs of her childhood, and buried her face in her hands.

"Go to your room." Michael stood up, repeating himself when she didn't move. "Your room,
Emma. Now."

I winced when she fled past me—as angry as
I was at her, I could hear the panic beneath her
sobs, and it was tough not to go after her and
gather her up in my arms.

Instead, I was surprised when Michael
tugged me upright and dragged me against him
to nuzzle his face in my hair.

"Welcome to the teen years, huh?" he

murmured. "I'm so sorry you went through that by yourself. And I'm… Well, I'm sorry we fought. I'm sorry about everything. I think I need to make a sign and wear it on my forehead from now on."

I fitted my body to his, breathing him in, winding my arms around his waist. "I'll get a matching one, then. I'm sorry you had to come home to this."

He pulled me with him onto the sofa and I laid my head on his shoulder. The windows behind the sofa were open to the soft day outside—the air was velvety and warm, green with growing things and the promise of real heat as the day wore on. I wanted nothing more than to sit right there, nestled into my husband, and pretend that everything was all right, that nothing had changed.

Michael had other ideas. "Is it this boy?"

"Jesse?" I angled my head up to look at him. "It's partly that. But I'm concerned she's making more of it than it is. That she's using him, in a way, as something to focus on instead of…well, everything else. It has to be weird for her, and then there's the idea that Drew might…die." I watched as he closed his eyes against the word, as if he seeing me say it was as bad as hearing it. "No one she knows has ever died before. No matter how she reacted at the beginning of all this, I think she's fascinated by the idea of a big brother."

Michael nodded. "I think so, too. I think she's confused and she's got all those hormones boiling over. But I don't know what Drew wants aside from, you know…not dying. God." He bit his bottom lip, worrying it with his teeth.

I followed his gaze as it wandered absently around the room. This was our haven, our home—the walls were the deep gray blue we'd argued over together, the woodwork a crisp, creamy white I'd taken days to paint. We'd bought the vintage carpet at an estate sale in Bucks County, and the books lining the shelves were an eclectic marriage of our taste. Everything in the room was familiar, loved, comforting, and nothing was as tempting as drawing the curtains and shutting out the rest of the world, with Michael beside me.

But for the first time, I couldn't read his eyes, aside from the anxiety that had appeared there weeks ago. I just couldn't tell which child worried him more—Emma or Drew. And I couldn't ask him. The list of things I couldn't bring myself to say was growing every minute.

"I could sleep for about a week," Michael murmured, idly stroking my hair. "I bet you could, too, after last night."

"Sleep will have to wait." I kissed his cheek and untangled myself to stand up. "If you can believe it, I have to go shopping this afternoon."

"For what?"

I sighed as I realized I would need to change out of the grubby jeans and old T-shirt I had been wearing since last night. "Bridesmaid dresses."

"ARE YOU SURE YOU WANT to do this today?" Nell asked as she parked the car at the mall two hours later. Despite the sunshine and the bright blue bowl of sky, the lot was packed.

"Are you?" I raised an eyebrow. "You were up pretty late, too, no thanks to me."

"Stop." She laid her hand on my arm. "I'm glad you called. And anyway, I'm used to the crazy hours at the hospital."

We climbed out of the car and she put her arm around me as we walked toward Lord & Taylor. "How is the prodigal daughter today?"

"Upset, furious, crying, pouting, guilty, confused—you name it." I shook my head. "I'm beginning to wish tranquilizer guns were an option."

Nell shifted her bag higher on her shoulder

and tucked a stray blond hair behind her ear. "And what's her punishment?"

"Grounded for two weeks, aside from school and the last-minute costume stuff for the play, and no phone in her room." I sighed and opened the door to the store, breathing in the cool air-conditioning. "She's not happy, that's for sure."

"Of course not," Nell agreed, and steered me past shoes toward women's dresses. "No phone in her room means no private commiseration with her friends or the infamous Jesse."

"Exactly." I angled a smile at Nell as she paused in front of a rack of floaty summer dresses.

"This is pretty." She held up a pale celadon tea-length dress with a stylish bateau neckline. She hesitated a moment, fingering the seed-pearl trim. "What about Michael?"

I stiffened as I reached for a delicate print dress in icy blue. No. Not now. I wanted to forget everything but dresses and Nell's wedding and very possibly a fruity, silly drink with an umbrella in it when we were done.

"Tess?"

I faced her, meeting her wide blue eyes. "He's tired. He's upset about Emma." I shrugged, then walked toward another rack, where I slid the hangers over the bar rougher than I should have.

She followed, the green dress still in her hand. "But how are you two…together?"

"Nell, please." I shook my head. "Please, can we not do this right now? I need an hour away from it. For weeks now it's been all I can think about, all anyone will talk about. I just…I want normal life back for one afternoon. Shopping with you. Lunch with you, if you're up for it. Maybe even some foofy, silly drink with an umbrella in it. Okay?"

Sympathy rippled across her face. Even though I hated to see it, hated to be the object of it, I accepted her one-armed hug with a smile. "Deal," she said. "Okay, seriously, what do you think of this one?" A wry grin twisted her mouth. "It's a lot better than the one you made me wear all those years ago."

My cheeks heated with embarrassment. "Hey, it was 1988. What do you want from me?"

"A little leeway twenty years from now when you look at pictures of my wedding." She laughed, and handed me the dress.

I took it and three others into the dressing room twenty minutes later while Nell browsed a few more racks. I'd promised to show her any of the dresses that really worked; Liza was a perfect size six, the bitch, and she'd agreed to let us choose whichever dress we liked.

I closed the door behind me and kicked off my sandals, peeled off my jeans and blouse and lifted the celadon dress over my head. After twisting around to zip it, I smoothed it over my hips and settled the skirt.

It was lovely, a good color against my skin. But I wasn't really focusing on it—instead, the image in the mirror was me in my wedding gown on a wet, cool April day. Hair bundled into a chignon under a simple tulle veil, Mom's pearl earrings and necklace my only jewelry aside from my engagement ring, I had stared at myself in the mirror in the small parlor beside the chapel at the First Presbyterian Church while I waited for the service to begin.

My mother had fussed with my veil while Nell leaned in to dust my cheekbones with blush one last time. I waved her away. "I'm blushing already," I said, and ducked. "Is it hot in here?"

"You're nervous." My mother straightened up and smiled at me in the mirror. She looked beautiful—her dress was the same slate-blue as her eyes, but it was the flicker of wistful sadness in them that struck me.

"Where's Michael?" I asked. The gray drizzle hadn't let up all day, and the glass was pearled with fat raindrops. The newly budded trees were silver with rain.

"You can't see him now," Nell chided me. Her shock was sweetly superstitious. "Just wait twenty minutes until the ceremony."

But I couldn't. Certainty burned inside me like the first star. I had to see him now, had to tell him how much I loved him before we parroted the words the minister would supply. I wanted to make my own vow to him, privately, and steal a little of his usual calm with a kiss before the ceremony began.

I was out of the room before Nell could dash after me, and found Michael in the choir room with my father and brothers. For a minute, I couldn't say a word—he was all elegance, long and dark and polished in his tuxedo. *My husband,* I thought, and felt the first prick of hot, happy tears.

"Tess, what are you doing?" my father protested, but Michael was already walking toward me, that slow, sure smile lighting his face. He followed me into the hall and closed the door behind him.

"This is supposed to be bad luck," he murmured, and leaned in to brush his lips against my cheek. "But I don't care. You are absolutely beautiful."

His hands were warm and strong over mine. If love could be felt that way, through the skin, in a touch, everything in his heart was there in his hands, an offering. I lifted my face to his. There was no stopping the tears now, makeup be damned. "I just had to tell you, now, while we're alone, how happy I am. That I love you. That I can't imagine anything I've ever wanted more than spending my life with you."

He searched my face so intently, those dark, dark eyes seeming to swallow me, my heart thudded. Did he see the truth of my words there? Did he believe me? But before I could say anything else, he lowered his mouth to mine and kissed me hard and long. I wound my arms around him as he whispered against my lips, "I love you more than anything, Tess. Always have, always will."

Our parents separated us like naughty children a moment later, shepherding us off to our separate rooms to wait for the signal that the ceremony was beginning. It did, just minutes later, and it went off exactly as we'd rehearsed, although I don't recall many of the details. I found myself staring at Michael through most of it, holding his hand as if I would float away should I let go. I do remember the moment we kissed, and my mother's face, blurred with tears, as Michael and I walked back down the aisle together, but the rest was a vague sense memory of roses, candlelight and a trill of adrenaline in my blood—

Nell knocked on the door of the dressing room, startling me out of memory, and I opened it to show her the single dress I'd tried on.

"Oh, that's really pretty on you," she breathed as she squeezed inside. "God, I would kill for your figure. What about the others?"

"I, um, haven't tried them on yet." Cue a sheepish smile. "Sorry. I was back at my wedding."

She rolled her eyes and sat down on the bench seat. "Focus, please. It's my turn! And I don't want it jinxed with all the rain you got."

"It didn't matter," I said, and let her unzip me. After stepping out of the dress, I hung it up and reached for the icy-blue one.

In the mirror, Nell smiled at me. "No, it didn't. It was a good day, wasn't it? I don't think I've ever seen Dad dance like that."

I laughed, remembering my father on the dance floor of the bed-and-breakfast where we'd held the reception, his bow tie loosened, a gin and tonic clutched in one hand. "He definitely had a good time, didn't he?"

"Everyone did." Nell shrugged, but her tone was fond when she added, "It's not hard to enjoy celebrating for two people who are pretty clearly meant for each other."

Meant for each other. It sounded good. That was the point of fairy tales, wasn't it? Destiny, soul mates, a future written in the stars. But on paper, Michael and I were very different. Reading and writing were his passions; my first love had been completely physical, an art form without words. Michael was pensive and compassionate and gentle; I was quick-tempered and impatient and scattered. He was content to be at home, surrounded by his books, settled in with me and Emma; I was usually eager to get out, see things, do things.

It was easy to believe that we were destined for each other when we fell in love so hard, so fast, when everyone who knew us was charmed by the pair that we became. But as I regarded myself in the mirror, the slim column of pale blue satin falling against my skin like water, I couldn't help wondering if Michael still felt the same way.

CHAPTER FOURTEEN

THE NEXT THREE DAYS WERE HELL, simply put. Emma slouched around the house either pouting or stonily silent. Every word out of her mouth was knife-edged, sharp with resentment or self-pity. I snapped at her, Michael snapped at me, and the moments we'd spent reconnecting on Saturday morning felt like something out of a naive fantasy. Even the weather was determined to be uncooperative—it was unreasonably warm for early June, and the heat made all of us sticky and ripe for arguments.

When the phone rang early Tuesday morning, I was unloading the dishwasher and cursing under my breath. Emma had left her French book on the kitchen table, and Michael had had another bad night's sleep, which meant I had, too. I was grouchy and fighting the beginning of a headache, neither of which made talking on the phone appealing.

I was surprised to hear Alicia Priest on the

other end—she had passed me a couple of photojournalism assignments over the years. She had worked for the *New York Times* before moving on to a big new lifestyle magazine, and the pieces I'd done for her had given me a few much appreciated artistic credentials.

"It's been ages," she said now, and I grabbed my mug of tea before sitting down. "How are you?"

"Busy," I said with a laugh. It wasn't a complete answer, but it would do. "Are you still at *HomeLife?*"

"Yes and no." I could hear her tapping on a keyboard in the background. "I've got something else going on, and while I know this is incredibly last minute, I wanted to ask if you were up for coming into the city today for lunch. My treat."

Without thinking, I glanced down at the disreputable pair of shorts and old T-shirt I'd pulled on that morning. I hadn't even showered yet. Lunch in Manhattan? Today?

But I hesitated for only a second. I hadn't been into the city in months, and at the moment the idea of a grown-up lunch with someone who had no interest in my personal life sounded like a tonic. "I could make the 11:45 train," I said, and began to grin. "Where do you want to meet?"

"A GALLERY?" I NEARLY choked on the ice water I'd swallowed. "You're opening a gallery?"

Alicia had snagged a window table at a trendy little Tuscan place uptown in the East Fifties, and she was waiting when I arrived. Sophisticated as ever in a creamy linen blouse and gray pants, her sleek dark hair bundled into a French twist, she looked as though she should have been the subject of a photo spread, not its editor. She lifted her shoulders with a sheepish, excited smile. "Not exactly. I mean, I'm not doing it alone. I have a partner. And a silent partner. And a money guy, and a lawyer…" She trailed off, laughing. "But what it comes down to is, yes, there's going to be a new gallery with my name on it."

"Alicia, that's incredible." I reached across the table and squeezed her hand before holding my glass up in a kind of toast. "Congratulations."

"Hold on there, miss," she warned me, and wagged her finger. "There's more."

I laughed. "Did you forget to tell me you won the lottery? Wait—you're marrying George Clooney."

"Sadly, no to both." She leaned closer, hazel eyes sparkling with mischief. "I want you to be part of our first exhibit."

Thank God I hadn't been drinking that time. The poor woman, not to mention the snowy tablecloth and chichi red dishes, would have been covered in ice water.

"Me, exhibit?" I breathed, my mind flipping through my catalog of photographs. Half of them were wedding proofs and family portraits. "Exhibit...what?"

"That's the thing." She beamed across the table at me, proud of herself. "I have a theme in mind, but it would be all new stuff. You could shoot to your heart's content all summer, and we could choose a set of twelve to eighteen shots when you're done."

The waiter appeared at the table then, young and stiffly formal in his white shirt and black tie, and we took a moment to order. I asked for the pollo alla diavola after Alicia ordered pasta with a name too complicated for me to remember, much less pronounce.

She was considering me with an expectant smile when the waiter walked away. "What do you think?"

"I think I'm speechless," I admitted. The tingle of excitement hadn't faded yet, and my mind was racing with possibilities. "I've never shown in a gallery. Well, not a Manhattan gallery. This is huge for me, Alicia, and I'm so grateful I can't think of what to say."

"Say you'll do it." She nodded when the

waiter appeared again, a bottle of wine in hand, and waited while he poured two glasses. "Your eye is fantastic, Tess, and I've been telling you for years you're wasting yourself on weddings and babies."

"Weddings and babies help pay the mortgage," I reminded her gently, but I couldn't help feeling a thrill of pride at her praise.

"I know." She sipped her wine carefully. "Ironically enough, I don't want you to stray too far from those subjects for the showing, either. *HomeLife* is sponsoring the opening, so we're creating a kind of tie-in theme. Homes and life, which is obviously pretty broad and might be covered by a few different artists. I'd like to see you do family."

Family. Of course. Was this some kind of karmic retribution? Was I being punished? A few weeks ago, I could have shot photos of a million different kinds of families with no sense of the surreal. The gay couple who'd bought the bookstore downtown and adopted a childless widow as their surrogate mother. Our neighbors, who had each been married before and whose children included a teenage son and daughter from their first unions, an energetic five-year-old boy they'd had together and a baby girl adopted from China. The family of women across town—grandmother, mother and two daughters—all living under the same roof. A few of Michael's college friends, each the victim of rough childhoods, who had become as close as siblings, a family by choice rather than blood.

I loved the fact that those kinds of families existed. That the notion of family was both flexible and durable, that it could expand to include people of all ages and colors and backgrounds but was, at its heart, what it had always been: a group of people who cared about and for one another.

And then my family had changed. We were four now instead of three, and five if I counted Sophia, which seemed only fair, even it was strange to contemplate. I didn't know if I was ready for us to be the sort of family I had always applauded.

"You don't like the idea." Alicia was crestfallen, and I realized how long I must have been musing about coincidence and karma.

"No, I do!" I picked up my wineglass and took a healthy swallow. "I think I'm still stunned, that's all."

"So you'll do it?" She was back to beaming, and lifted her glass in anticipation.

I clinked mine against hers with a delicate

ping. There was no question, not really. A gallery exhibit in New York? The chance to shoot photos that didn't have to include a groom peeling off his bride's garter or hide a toddler's teary cheeks? This was photography on a whole new level, one I'd been trying to climb to for years. "You better believe I'll do it."

DURING MY JUNIOR YEAR in college, Michael took the train to New York on the Tuesday evening before Thanksgiving. We were going to spend the day together before heading home late Wednesday afternoon.

"Spend the *night* together, you mean," Jane teased. She was packing to go home herself, randomly tossing clothes into a duffel bag. Carter had agreed to bunk in with Marissa that night, since Sydney had already left for Ohio.

"Day, night, whatever," I said with an airy wave, but I was grinning. We would spend nearly every minute of the weekend together at home, but "nearly" wasn't quite enough when we couldn't sleep together. Last year had involved CIA-level planning in order for us to make love once. Stealing an hour away from the assembled families and then staking out a private space seemed to get more difficult every year.

"Well, enjoy it." Jane flopped on her bed and propped her chin in her hands. "Think of me once in a while, will you? Up in Connecticut with my horrible cousins and my grandmother's disgusting candied yams and no luscious boyfriend to distract me."

I rolled my eyes and sat cross-legged on the floor beside her bed. She had broken up with her latest boyfriend, an economics major from Florida, just a week earlier. Even though she and Carter and I had decided he was a shit with no sense of humor and had a really weird affection for country music, Jane claimed he was good in bed.

"You'll survive," I told her, then picked up a hank of her thick auburn hair and flicked her cheek with it. "I hear curvy redheaded history majors are all the rage this year."

She snorted, but she smiled just the same. Jane was never without a boyfriend for long. Keeping a particular guy around was a different story, but I had to give the girl credit for her perseverance.

Two hours later she stretched up on tiptoe to kiss Michael's cheek when he arrived, and then slung her bag over her shoulder and took off for Grand Central. Then I was enveloped in Michael's arms, and it was hours before we

came up for air and decided to dress and go out
to find something to eat.

We held hands as we walked across the park
in the chilly night air. It was a cold November,
raw and wet, and the stars were faint, gritty
smudges of light in the dark sky. I unwound my
scarf as we walked into a pizza place on
Bleecker Street, and let Michael order slices
and sodas for both of us.

"Next year visiting won't be so complicated,"
I said when we had settled in one of the tiny
booths. "With Marissa and Sydney gone, Carter
and Jane and I are going to look for an apartment.
I already told Mom and Dad, and they agreed to
give me money for rent. God, I can't wait. I'm so
sick of the dorm I can't even tell you."

He didn't say anything for a minute, but his
eyes were busy searching my face. "I was going
to ask you about that," he said finally, and put
down the slice of pizza he'd already half
devoured. "I was thinking about applying to
graduate school…"

I nodded, confused, my mouth full. That had
always been his plan.

"Here, in New York," he went on. In the
crowded bustle of the pizza parlor, his voice
was so soft I wasn't sure I'd heard him right,
but there was no mistaking the hope in his eyes.

"I want to apply to NYU and Columbia. I thought we could get an apartment together. Live together."

I knew what I should have felt, what Michael no doubt expected me to feel: elation, excitement, joy. Instead, my heart squeezed in panic.

Senior year would be tough—Carter and Jane and I all had decisions to make, courses to pass, résumés to write. An apartment with my dorm mates was supposed to be the saving grace, an exercise in adulthood, a taste of freedom, with shared clothes, shared bills and one another's company as a safety net.

I was taking too long to answer—already Michael's brow had furrowed in concern. "We're going to do it eventually," he said, and I ignored the faint note of betrayal in his voice. "This way we wouldn't have to wait. We could find something really cheap if it was just the two of us, and then we could be together all the time." I watched his Adam's apple bob as he swallowed, and then he aimed his next shot. "Like tonight, Tess. Just like tonight, but every day."

The little shop was overheated, and I had to fight the urge to run outside, where I could drink in the cold, damp air. "Michael…"

"You don't look happy about this." He raked a hand through his hair and shoved his paper plate away. "I thought you would be. Happy, I mean. I thought this was the plan."

"It *is* the plan." The words escaped in an angry hiss, and I sat back and took a deep breath, waiting for my heart to stop its furious thumping. "It is. But I thought you were going to do your master's at Harvard. I thought I was going to come up to Boston after I graduate…" Miserable, I let the idea trail off unfinished. Michael looked as if I'd slapped him.

Love wasn't supposed to be this hard, was it? And I did love Michael. But he was always one step ahead of me, his gaze fixed somewhere in a future I hadn't even imagined yet, and pulling me along behind him like a hesitant child.

I had never questioned that we would stay together, get married, but I had never taken the time to puzzle out the details, and now Michael had settled us in a little apartment together. He probably knew which subway he would take if he was accepted to Columbia instead of NYU, had decided whether he liked Gristedes better than D'Agostino's, and just how much money we would have for groceries every week.

For a moment, staring across the table at the grim set of his jaw, the dark hair falling across his forehead as he focused on the scarred linoleum tabletop, I felt my blood run cold. "Did you already apply here in the city?"

He slid out of the booth and shrugged on his coat, but not before I saw how deeply I had cut him. His eyes were empty, bottomless. "No. And don't worry, I won't."

We slept together in my single bed that night, but Michael faced the wall, his bare back to me. A mere six inches separated us, but we had never been as far apart as we were that night.

I FELT THE SAME THING NOW, sitting beside him on the train home from New York. Our shoulders bumped companionably as the train rattled over the tracks, but we rode in silence.

I had called Michael the minute Alicia and I said goodbye outside the restaurant, and I'd taken the subway down to his office. It was already two o'clock, and I'd asked my mother to check in on Emma when she got home from school. I was still buzzing, excited to tell him about Alicia's offer, and as the six train sped through the tunnels on the way to Union Square, I was already imagining the series of photographs I would shoot.

"Hi, there," he said when I was shown into his office, and stood up to kiss me. But the gesture felt rote, and as flat as his eyes were. His tie was loose, and his hair stood up in wild tufts, as if he'd spent the past few hours combing his fingers through it carelessly.

"What's wrong?" I moved a pile of galleys off the single guest chair in the room and sat down. Schuyler and Lansing was a prestigious small publisher, but like every prestigious small publisher, the firm was more concerned with reviews and literary awards than the comfort of their offices. Michael's was located at the far end of a rabbit's warren, and about the size of a walk-in closet.

"I was going to tell you later." He leaned on the edge of his desk, threatening to topple a stack of manuscripts, and folded his arms over his chest. "I got the results of the bone marrow testing today. I'm not a match."

The words struck deep—to the bone, it seemed in that moment. All I could think about was Emma, my baby, my little girl, and possibly Drew's last hope.

But I heard myself saying, "Oh, sweetheart, I'm sorry." I got up and went to put my arms around him. He was stiff, his arms still crossed, and under my lips his cheek felt too warm. He was holding it all in, the disappointment and anger and fear, and it was burning up inside him.

"What did the doctor say?" I shoved the manuscripts away and sat beside him, my arm around his back.

"The doctor didn't call." He shook his head, as if the words were too difficult to utter. "Drew did."

I made some kind of soft noise—I heard it in the quiet room, knew it had come from my throat, but I was far away, imagining what it must be like to tell your father he couldn't save you. To be facing the end of the road at twenty, a lifetime of things not yet experienced.

Michael got up and paced across the little room, and before I could utter another word, he asked, "What are you doing in the city, anyway? Did I know you were coming in?"

He was trying so hard to keep himself together—I was pretty sure if I touched him again now, he would split open, all of the stress and confusion pouring out of him in a heated rush. So I sat where I was, carefully glancing out the window while he ran his hand over his forehead. "It was a spur-of-the-moment thing," I said. "Alicia Priest asked me in to have lunch."

"That's nice." He was already gone, lost in his thoughts, moving back around his desk to sit down.

All I could do was nod as he sifted through the pages of a manuscript he'd been reading when I walked in. Now wasn't the time to share my good news, but a part of me was angry that I had to wait. *A selfish part,* I told myself firmly. *A small, unworthy part.*

But that part of me was getting restless. Too many things were going unsaid, and the weight of them was getting heavier by the day.

I convinced him to leave the office early, at least, but I couldn't help comparing the trip home with others we had taken. If we were together in the city, we usually stopped off for a drink somewhere decadent, or grabbed dirty water dogs from one of the vendors near Penn Station, feeding them to each other laden with mustard and ketchup and onions until we were both laughing at the mess. Today we rode the subway to the station in silence, and waited as if we were strangers for our train to be announced.

Of course I didn't blame Michael for being upset about the test results. Michael was the sort who scooped up spiders with a piece of paper and carried them outside, and dropped his spare change in collection tins for needy sick kids everywhere he saw one. He would give an arm and both legs, and probably more, to keep Emma and me alive.

But I didn't want just part of him. I wanted all of him, the Michael I had loved for so long, to look at me again. And I didn't think he knew it.

CHAPTER FIFTEEN

On Thursday afternoon Emma was peeling potatoes for dinner, under my direction, and making a mess. Being grounded had seriously restricted her free-time options, and I realized she was bored when she offered to help with dinner. "I got another e-mail from Drew today," she said idly, and flicked a piece of wet skin into the sink.

I looked up from the table, where I had spread a stack of old photos. Baby Emma and my five-year-old self were side by side amid pictures of my parents, wedding photos and snapshots of me holding Emma and my mom toting me on her hip.

An e-mail from Drew? *Another* e-mail from Drew?

"We exchanged addresses when we were in Cambridge," Emma added before I could say a word. "We've been e-mailing back and forth since then."

I let this news settle in by getting up to find a

pot for the potatoes. There was nothing to be upset about. Drew was, after all, Emma's half brother, and even though I'd met him only once, I thought I could trust him not to engage her in inappropriate conversation. But their correspondence was another proof of Emma's independence, and she clearly loved the fact that she had surprised me with it.

"What do you two talk about?" I made my tone as light as possible as I showed her how to slice the potatoes into manageable chunks.

"Stuff." She rubbed her nose with the back of her forearm and blew a piece of hair out of her eyes. "I ask him stuff about growing up, and he tells me. Sometimes he asks me the same kinds of things."

I didn't reply. I wasn't sure where this conversation was going, and I couldn't pry. I didn't want to be caught prying, at least. But it was impossible not to wonder if Drew had asked what Michael had been like as a dad, and if he resented the fact that he hadn't had one when he was a child.

Poor little kid had to have wondered who his father was, I thought, watching Emma slicing the potatoes, her brow furrowed as she sectioned off chunks. What child wouldn't, especially when he trotted off to kindergarten and discovered almost all his friends had a mommy *and* a daddy?

And what had Sophia told him about his lack of a father? That his father was dead? Surely she wouldn't have told a six- or seven-year-old that she didn't know who his father was.

Emma's tongue was out, resting on her upper lip, a sure sign of concentration. I had taken pictures of her doing the same thing, completely unaware, when she was little and furiously working in one of her coloring books, or trying to tie her shoes. In fact, one of the pictures on the kitchen table showed her curled in Michael's lap, just the tip of her tongue visible between her lips as he read to her from *The Little House in the Big Woods.*

I had never doubted that Michael would be a good father. As early as the first summer we met, I had observed him with his sister, Melissa, then a slightly annoying eight-year-old, and marveled at his patience with her. He didn't simply tolerate her; he enjoyed spending time with her. His face softened when he listened to her chattering about her new friends or the mean boy who had teased her at the pool, and the sight of it always sent a flicker of warmth through me.

When I found out I was pregnant with Emma,

it was Michael who had whooped and danced. I had always wanted kids, but in an unspecified "someday" kind of way. That a child was definitely on the way, no turning back barring disaster, was suddenly so terrifying I had ended up on the kitchen floor, breathing into a paper bag while Michael rubbed my back and kissed my hair.

Embarrassing, to say the least. But for the first time, I seemed to be the one looking further down the road than Michael was. Babies— newborns—were one thing. They were a few months of sleeplessness and crying and lots of laundry. Children were forever. Children grew out of hand-holding and bedtime kisses, and talked back and picked their noses. Children argued and wanted things that were dangerous and bad for them, and went to high school and drove too fast and didn't always study, and then became adults who would still regard us as Mom and Dad, especially when it came to borrowing money.

"You're a glass-half-empty person sometimes, aren't you?" Michael had said with a laugh, sliding down to sit beside me on the kitchen floor of our little New York apartment. An apartment, I had also pointed out, that was really too small for us already, even without baby equipment.

In bed that night, as I lay on my back, he'd stroked my still nicely flat belly and listed all the wonderful things children were. He'd told funny stories about his own childhood, and asked me to tell him some of mine. I'd fallen asleep with the warmth of his palm shielding the tiny embryo inside me, and the sound of his voice in my ear as steady as a waterfall.

"Mom? How much water?"

I glanced up to find Emma staring at me, eyebrows raised. She'd finished cutting the potatoes and had piled them in the pot.

"Just enough to cover them completely," I said, and felt myself blushing as the rest of the memory pushed to the surface. Later that same night I had woken up, calm and completely alert, to find a stripe of moonlight across Michael's face as he slept, illuminating the curve of his cheek. And the rush of love that swept through me then was so huge, so complete, I'd reached for him, waking him with my mouth so I could slide on top of him. Still drowsy but powerfully aroused, he'd smiled up at me while I rode him, and he laid his hands on my belly as he watched me fly.

"Mom, what is your deal?" Emma complained. She had the pot on the flame already, and was waving a lid in my face. "Are you, like, on drugs today or what?"

"I most certainly am not," I protested, but I knew my cheeks were pink. I was living in my head so often these days, just like Michael, that memories I hadn't thought about in years were coming back. Clearly, I needed to avoid the sexy ones when Emma was around. "Turn the heat down a little and put the lid on."

She did as I asked and then wandered over to the table, where she picked up a picture of herself at age two, giggling wildly, her hair in pigtails and evidence of a half-eaten chocolate-chip cookie all over her face. "What's all this for?"

I hesitated. I still hadn't told Michael about the exhibit, and I wasn't about to spill the beans to Emma first. He'd closeted himself in his little office when we got home Tuesday night, and he'd still been turtled up yesterday, drawn and exhausted.

"Just sorting through old photos," I said, wiping up the counter where the potato skins had left a wet, starchy mess. "Nothing special."

She held up another picture, this one of her sometime in kindergarten. "I was pretty cute, huh?"

I smiled at her. "You really were. I used to call you Button for that very reason."

Her mouth went slack for a minute, but then

a light went on. "I remember that! God, Mom, that was embarrassing."

I rolled my eyes. "Of course."

She was lingering, sifting through the pictures with idle fingers, and I could tell she had something on her mind. Barefoot, in a pair of her oldest jeans and a simple pink T-shirt, she'd skinned her hair back in a ponytail after school. Her shoulder blades stuck out from her back like a pair of fragile wings.

I took a London broil out of the fridge and cut open the plastic wrap to season it. If she wanted to talk, I would be ready, but I wasn't going to push her. This interval of peace was too rare right now, and too pleasant to risk shattering. Maybe Drew had given her some big-brother advice about dealing with consequences, or about acting like a grown-up if she expected to be treated like one.

"I told Drew what Dad was like when I was little. How he used to read to me, and made me that fort in the backyard and all," Emma said finally. She sat on one of the chairs, her bare feet on the seat and her arms wrapped around her legs. She lifted her eyes to mine when I turned around. "Do you think that was…okay? I mean, he asked and all."

There she was, my little girl, the one who was

still unsure of herself, who longed to please, who believed in happy endings. "I think it's great, honey," I said as I took olive oil, vinegar and grill seasoning out of the cabinet. Keeping the conversation casual was the smart thing to do. "I'm sure he has a lot of questions."

"Yeah." She came to stand behind me, peering over my shoulder as I seasoned the meat. "We were talking about what Christmas was like, what we did in the summer, stuff like that. He's really smart, Mom. And so cool. He's…well, he's a lot like Dad, I guess."

I glanced back at her and smiled. "That's a good thing to be, don't you think?"

Her grin was lopsided. "Yeah." She was quiet for a moment before she added, "But it sucks that Dad's bone marrow didn't match."

I waited, concentrating on the bottle of seasoning in my hand, but while she didn't go on, she didn't move, either. Waiting for me to weigh in. I had no wisdom to offer, but I was concerned, and I hoped she understood that. I wanted to find out how much she knew about the process, or if she had an inkling that we might ask her to be tested. "What can his doctors do now? Did he mention anything?"

She might as well have pulled a shade down over her face. The vulnerable, worried child was gone, and a shuttered young woman stood before me, instead, lips pursed, eyes guarded. "There are things," she said absently. "I'm, um, not exactly sure. What else can I do here?"

"I've got it, thanks." I'd been moody as a teenager, but Emma's mood swings were giving me whiplash. "What's with your newfound interest in cooking, anyway?"

She rolled her eyes. "I'm trying to be helpful, Mother. *Responsible*. Isn't that what you're always telling me to be?"

"Sorry. You're right," I said, and shook my head as she headed upstairs, a fresh can of diet soda in hand. If she thought I believed that, maybe I could sell *her* a bridge.

I didn't have much time to wonder about her abrupt about-face, though. The phone rang a moment later, and it was Michael.

"Can you pack a bag for me?" he asked. "I'm catching the next train home, and I've got a ticket on a seven o'clock flight to Boston tonight."

"What…?" He was going too fast, and the panic in his voice was contagious. I stood in the middle of the kitchen, frozen, watching as the pot of potatoes on the stove began to boil over. "Michael, what happened?"

"Sophia called. Drew's in the hospital." He

sounded harried, a bit breathless, and I could hear the rush of traffic through the phone. If he was on his cell, he was probably already on his way to the train station. "Something about neutropenia and an infection...I'm not sure what it all means, but he collapsed this morning at the library. I told her I would come."

"Of course." I moved the pot off the flame and headed upstairs, the portable phone wedged between my ear and my shoulder. "I'll pack some things for you now. How long will you be gone?"

"I don't know, honey." A horn blared, and Michael swore under his breath. "Use your best judgment, okay?"

He hung up before I even had a chance to say goodbye.

I KNEW YOU WOULD be okay.

That was what Michael had said when he left for the airport Thursday evening, and the words echoed in my head Saturday morning as I searched through the piles of paper on his desk for the electric bill.

Was I okay? I wasn't falling apart—I couldn't. I had a child and a home and a career to take care of—and I wasn't the one whose child was dying, for one thing.

I was the one who had a wedding to photograph this afternoon, and who had remembered the electric bill hadn't been paid yet, and whose resentful teenager had been storming around since she'd heard her father was flying to Boston, because she wanted to go with him.

"He *is* my brother," she'd argued, stationed in the doorway to our bedroom as Michael looked through the things I had packed for him. "I might want to see him, too, you know? God, Daddy, what if he's really dying?"

The horror on Michael's face in that moment had spoken volumes, and even I had winced when he said, "Yes, Emma. What if that happens? Do you think that matters more to you than it does to him?"

As of Friday afternoon, Drew had been stable, at least, but his compromised immune system was not yet up to the job of fighting a respiratory infection. It was all so needless, so awful— that a bright, loving kid who hadn't even graduated college yet might die of what was essentially a chest cold because the chemotherapy to battle his leukemia was a kind of poison.

I'd never wanted to scream so often in my life. Shattering a couple of cheap dishes against the driveway was beginning to tempt me. I wanted to curse at everything and everyone. Sophia, for keeping Drew a secret from Michael. Michael, for caring so very much. Drew, for being ill. Emma, for being a teenager. Cancer, for existing.

But most of all, I wanted to scream at myself, for letting Michael go all those years ago, for opening the door to this tangled skein of lives and emotions.

And of course, I couldn't do that. I had a wedding to go to and an electric bill to find.

I was wrapped in a light summer robe, the heavy mass of my hair still wet against my back as I searched the surface of Michael's desk for the bill. We split up the chore most of the time, which was a spectacularly stupid way to run a household, and this month we'd both been too preoccupied to keep track of what had been paid when. Only when I'd checked the calendar this morning had the date rung a bell, and I was petrified that if I didn't mail off a check when I left the house, we'd wake up a few days from now with no power.

It wasn't as if Michael would ordinarily attend the wedding with me, or as if Emma needed a babysitter. But I wasn't used to surprise trips, and that same small, unworthy part of me bristled at his words: *I knew you'd be okay.* Okay with what? That he was taking off to visit the son he'd never known until a few weeks ago? That he was taking off at all? That he was staying in his ex-lover's apartment while they worried together over their son dying?

Why would he so blithely assume that I was okay with any of it, much less all of it? The only answer I could reach, the one had that had kept me awake Thursday night until the only thing left on TV was infomercials, was that he didn't believe I loved him enough to be bothered.

In my heart, I knew Michael didn't feel that way. But I couldn't erase the memory of that moment, sprawled in bed, the TV flickering across the darkened room, Walter snoring beside me on the mattress, that my head had offered up the thought. And the panic had been a fist in my gut.

I didn't have time to agonize over it now, of course, and I shouldn't have been agonizing at all. But as I sifted through the assorted papers on Michael's desk, my fingers skimmed over a yellow legal tablet, half hidden under an article clipped from the newspaper and a credit card offer. The top page was covered with Michael's precise, upright hand.

He'd written a letter to Drew. Or started one,

at least. And even though it was none of my business, I pulled the tablet from the pile and sat down in his desk chair to read it.

Drew:

I'm not sure how to begin. There are things I'd like to tell you, things I'd like you to know, and when you first contacted me, I thought we would have plenty of time to cover all of them. There are things I'd like to know, too, memories of your childhood only you can tell me, and I hope I have a chance to hear them.

I'm sorrier than I can say that I didn't have a chance to share any of those years with you. I understand your mom had reasons for her decision to keep me out of your life, and I have to respect that. Now that we've met, however, I'd like to get to know you. I'm not sure if I can be a father to a young man who has grown up so well already, and I don't know if you want that kind of relationship with me, but I'd like for us to be friends if we can.

I don't know how much your mom has told you about our relationship. I'm not sure if you want my feelings about it, but as it's the only detail of your life—its very

beginning, at least—that I can offer, I will.
I hope you don't mind.

As the last sentence sank in, I swallowed
hard. I didn't have time to sit and read the letter,
and anyway, I had no place reading it all.
Michael had given me the bare-bones version
of his relationship with Sophia, and I hardly
needed to torture myself with the details. But
I couldn't help myself—I couldn't bring
myself to ask Michael about those months he
had spent with her, but it didn't mean I wasn't
curious about how he had met her, what he had
seen in her that he couldn't resist—what she
had been able to offer him, all those years ago,
that I couldn't.

I met your mom in the laundry room of
the apartment building I had just moved
into. She was wearing old jeans and a
T-shirt with a caricature of Jane Austen on
the front, but the first thing I really noticed
was her eyes. They were so very dark, and
that day they seemed to be laughing—at
me, at my odd collection of dirty clothes,
at my frustration with the washer that
wouldn't take my quarters without a fight.
She was so calm, so self-possessed, that I

couldn't believe there was anything she couldn't do if she set her mind to it.

I'm sure you're thinking, you got all that from an hour doing laundry together? No, not quite, but my first impression proved to be true the longer I knew her. I loved it when she spoke to me in Italian, I loved to watch her paint, and she kindly listened to me as I rambled on about the stories I was writing, and the literature I was studying in my first year of graduate school. It was late spring, and I had decided to stay in Boston for the summer, which I had never done before. Part of the reason for that decision was a serious rift between Tess and me, and your mother—also very kindly—sat through hours of me pouring out all my anger and sense of betrayal.

I'm not sure how much you want me to say about this. There are a million details I could supply—nights spent eating Chinese takeout on the floor of the shabby little apartment I was sharing with a roommate, the summer day your mother and I took the bus to the beach, with a picnic lunch she had packed, the rainy weekend we spent at an art house theater during a William Wyler retrospective. But none of those details tell the whole story of what we shared.

I can tell you this, though. Your mother meant a lot to me, and I respected her—her passion for her art, her ironclad streak of practicality, her generosity and compassion, her enormous heart. There are other things that I loved about her, of course, things that are too private to outline here. I don't regret breaking things off with her, because I wanted another chance to make things work between Tess and me, but I know...

I couldn't believe it. He hadn't finished the letter. Heart pounding, I stared at the trailing sentence, the words that might lead to a hundred different places. What did he know? That he loved me more than Sophia? That Sophia would be all right on her own? That he couldn't have us both?

The unwritten answer to that question was something to hold on to as I went back upstairs to dress, electric bill in hand. If I didn't focus on that, I would have to think about what my husband had said about loving another woman.

CHAPTER SIXTEEN

"HE'S HOME," EMMA SHOUTED from the front porch Monday at dinnertime. I walked into the hall as she ran barefoot down the walk to the cab that had pulled up to the curb in the velvet twilight. Walter pressed his nose to the screen door, waiting, his tail thumping wildly.

My heart was beating just as frantically, but anticipation wasn't the reason. For the first time, I was almost frightened to see Michael. Our phone calls over the weekend had been brief, and Michael had been distracted every time we talked, full of words and numbers that I didn't understand, white-blood-cell counts and liver function and blood-oxygen levels.

A foreign language to me, as foreign as this strange apprehension about facing my husband after days apart. I couldn't forget Michael's letter to Drew—the ink seemed to have stained my fingers, indelible, leaving me to carry the words around for days.

Emma threw her arms around him as the cab pulled away, and he punctuated a one-armed hug with a kiss on her forehead. "How's my little girl?" he asked as they walked up to the house. Her answer was to rest her head against his shoulder and keep her arm tight around his waist as they mounted the front steps.

"And how's my big girl?" Michael asked me. He dropped his suitcase on the dusty porch floor and gave Emma a nudge into the house, watching me, waiting for me to say something.

Tears were a hot, sudden pressure in my eyes, and dangerously close to spilling. Michael looked so good to me, and yet he looked so awful at the same time, exhausted and distracted and too thin. All I wanted to do was throw myself into his embrace as Emma had done, but if I did that, I was afraid the tangled knot of confusion and fear inside me would unravel.

I let him take my hand, tug me toward him, and the taste of him when he kissed me was so comforting, so familiar, I couldn't resist running one finger along his jaw. He hadn't shaved in a day or two. "I'm okay," I murmured. "How about you?"

"Exhausted." He reached for his bag, and we went into the house together. "It's been a long couple of days."

Emma was waiting in the kitchen, where I had made a meat loaf despite the heat. It was Michael's favorite.

"So how is he, Dad?" she said. She'd painted her toenails purple earlier in the afternoon, and beneath the overhead light they resembled fat, ripe grapes. "Really. Is he going to be okay?"

Michael sat down heavily at the kitchen table, and I opened the fridge to grab him a beer. As he twisted off the cap, he met Emma's steady gaze. "I don't know, honey. He's out of danger right now, but he needs a bone marrow transplant to have any chance of surviving more than a couple of months."

I braced for tears, but instead, Emma nodded slowly. Her eyes were troubled, but something about the set of her jaw wasn't right. I'd seen that determination in her before, and I could only hope she knew that sheer force of will wouldn't keep Drew alive.

She didn't disappoint me, either. During dinner, she put down her glass of water and faced Michael and me across the table, most of her meat loaf untouched on her plate, her fries cold and limp. "Can I ask for a favor?"

This will be interesting, I thought. I wasn't prepared to lift her punishment for the prom-night stunt even if her half brother was terminally ill, and I was already angry to think that she would use Drew as leverage to ask for special treatment.

But she surprised me again. "I know I'm grounded, but I wanted to ask if Jesse could come for dinner tomorrow night. I mean, I was the one who decided to stay out on prom night, not him. I'm the one who screwed up. I can't let you think he's a bad influence or something." Her face was bright with hope, and when I glanced at Michael, he had nearly choked on a piece of meat loaf.

"Dinner?" His eyes were wide. "Um, Tess, is that okay with you?"

Wasn't it too early for her to bring a boy to dinner to meet the parents so formally? That newly familiar fist of panic squeezed again. Everything was still changing, including Emma, and I didn't know how to make it stop.

But I didn't know how to deny her, either. Being grounded should have meant friends weren't allowed to visit, but I was glad that she had at least asked, instead of springing him on us. Maybe she deserved a little consideration for trying to go about something the right way.

And if she was serious about this boy, as I was beginning to suspect, we needed to know him better.

"It's okay with me," I said finally, suddenly aware that I was still holding a French fry halfway to my mouth. "But don't expect anything gourmet."

"Mom." She laughed. "As if. Although I would love it if you made your special pasta and that herb bread. I bet Jesse would love it."

Really. I could only hope my mouth wasn't hanging open as she cleared her plate without a reminder and hugged me before she left the room in search of her homework.

"She must really like this kid," Michael murmured as we listened to her setting up in the next room, humming something. "I don't think I'm ready for this."

I gave him a sympathetic smile. Life moved faster these days, and kids grew up quicker. Sex hadn't been scandalous between seventeen-year-olds when we were in high school. Did that mean that now, at fifteen, it was completely acceptable? I shuddered. "You and me both, babe."

Emma's request was a perfect distraction, though. As concerned as I was about her relationship with Jesse, it gave Michael and me something to focus on aside from Drew, and the unanswered questions I had nearly convinced myself not to ask. If I squinted and angled my head, I could almost see the three of us as we had seemed to be only weeks ago, and the image was a comforting one. I could hold on to it if I tried, and by the time we were finished eating I had decided that I had upset myself for nothing. Michael loved me. Michael knew I loved him.

As I scraped our plates and loaded the dishwasher, I repeated the words to myself. I didn't need to ask him anything just to soothe my own wounded ego. He was tired, and understandably stressed. Drew's appearance in our lives may have rocked the boat, but I wasn't about to tip it over with ridiculous insecurities.

It was a gorgeous night, too. The day's heat had faded into a warm breeze, and when I took Walter out, the stars were thick and bright in the sky. I unclipped Walter's leash and gave him his biscuit, tonight wasn't for conversation, especially not an awkward one. If I wanted Michael to know how much I loved him, I had a better way to show him.

I turned off the lights downstairs and locked up early. Emma had retreated to her room, and Michael was already upstairs, too. I found him sprawled in bed, naked under the sheet, idly flipping through the mail he'd carried up with him.

"You paid the electric bill?" he said without

looking up, and I smiled. Even distracted, unshaven and tired, he was beautiful. The stubble along his jaw gave him a slightly dangerous air, and despite the weight he'd lost, his body was still hard, the muscles in his shoulders and his abdomen still defined. Desire flickered inside me, a hungry tongue of flame, and I started to undress before I answered.

"I did," I said, and pulled off my shirt, unhooked my bra and let it drop to the floor. Michael always slept naked, even in the dead of winter, but I usually wore a T-shirt. He'd noticed, too—when I turned off the lamp on the night table and got into bed, leaving only the TV's faint glow to light the room, I thought I heard a husky rumble in his throat.

"I missed you," I said, sliding in next to him and running my hand along his thigh. The hair was bristly under my fingertips, and the muscle there stiffened in response to my teasing touch.

The mail fell to the floor when I moved closer, rustling the sheet, hooking my bare leg over his and laying my cheek against his chest. There it was, the heartbeat that had lulled me to sleep so many times, the rhythm as familiar as my own. His arm came around me, and his hand stroked idly over my ass.

My fingers found him already hard, a pulse of

arousal in the vein that ran the length of his erection. But when I turned my face up to kiss him, he wasn't there. His mouth moved under mine, his tongue was hot against my lips, but his mind was somewhere else, somewhere other than our bed and the sweet friction of our bodies.

I could change that. At least, I hoped I could. I flicked my tongue over the flat disk of his nipple, rubbed his calf with my foot, but I got only a vague grunt in reply. "What's wrong?" I whispered, but a part of me was panicking already, because I knew the answer.

"I'm sorry, babe." He kissed the top of my head, but he was already shifting away, sitting up. "I'm just preoccupied about Drew. And Sophia."

Something inside me broke. A dam opening, maybe, a precarious floodgate that had so far held all my confusion and fear safely inside. They poured out as I wrenched away from him, and before I knew it, I was asking him, "Why? *Why?*"

He was stunned. "Why am I preoccupied? Because Drew's dying, in case you hadn't heard."

I stumbled out of bed, ashamed for him to see the tears on my cheeks. "Not that," I snapped as I grabbed up the T-shirt I had left sitting on the bed. "Why did you sleep with her? How could you?"

The words seemed to hang in midair, flashing

like a neon sign, and just as harsh and inevitable. I hadn't realized how unbearable the weight of them inside me had become, but now that they were out, hovering between us unanswered, I would have taken them back if I could. How could anything Michael said now possibly make me feel better?

He swung his legs out of the bed, and his feet hit the floor with a dangerous thud. The outrage rippling across his face was huge and hot, and I flinched when he stalked toward me. He hadn't even bothered to put on a pair of shorts.

"How could *I* do it?" He grabbed my arm when I looked away from the shock of betrayal in his eyes. "How can you even ask me that? You're the one who said it was over. You fucking drove to Cambridge to tell me in person. '*Over*,' you said. How was I supposed to know you'd change your mind?"

It was true. I'd known it all along. But hearing it from Michael, who was angrier than I could recall him ever being, was more painful than anything I'd felt.

I couldn't even speak. I sank to the floor, the fringed edge of the carpet rough under one bare thigh, and vaguely wondered if Emma could hear us. It didn't seem to matter, though—I couldn't imagine that the room, the house, the world, could bear Michael's fury. Any minute we would both shatter into pieces, too small and broken to repair, and the world with us.

He wasn't finished, either. He paced the room, still unabashedly naked, the blue light of the TV reflected in his dark eyes, the hair that fell across his forehead.

"Do you know what it did to me when you told me you were ending it?" he demanded. "Do you have any idea? I loved you from the moment I met you, Tess. I gave you everything I had. But you weren't sure, you wanted time or space or whatever goddamn thing it was, and I gave it to you. I gave it to you!"

This last was punctuated with his hand smacking the top of my dresser, and I flinched again, not even trying to hide my tears now.

"What I found with Sophia was comfort, not revenge. And not love. Not at first," he said. He ran his hands through his hair restlessly as he paced the room again. "I didn't know you would change your mind! All I knew was that I missed you, and I still loved you so much. And when you called that day, when you asked me to come back, I jumped. I fucking *jumped* at it, Tess. Doesn't that count for anything?"

I managed to nod, and a moment later he dropped to the floor beside me and gathered me against his bare chest. My cheeks were wet and flushed, and his cool skin was a blessing as he rocked me.

"Love is a choice, Tess." His voice had softened, too. "It's a choice you make every day. I didn't choose our separation—you did. Maybe I should have lived like a monk, but for how long? I had no idea how long it would last, and I was pretty sure it was supposed to be forever. I needed someone, Tess. I needed comfort."

He set me away from him, just far enough to meet my eyes. "That day you drove away from Cambridge, I'd lost the one person I'd ever loved completely. And the hell of it was, I never stopped loving you. Even when I was with Sophia, it was you I was thinking about. Don't you know that? Doesn't the way I came back to you mean anything?"

I still couldn't answer—I was crying too hard, huge, gulping sobs that shook me to the core. Because I finally understood something that had puzzled me since the weekend we got back together, and the truth of it made me even guiltier than ever.

MICHAEL TOOK THE TRAIN down to New York the day after I called him and said I wanted to see him, wanted us to get back together. Jane's boyfriend was in town from Wisconsin, so the apartment Jane and Carter and I shared that year was going to be cramped—far too small for five adults, four of whom would need privacy. Carter was willing to pack a bag and camp out on someone's couch for the weekend, but Michael had other ideas. Within minutes, we were on the subway uptown and checking into a hotel on Tenth Avenue that was little more than a motor inn. After an hour inside the stale, none-too-clean room, I understood why.

He'd never undressed himself, or me, so quickly, I thought later. He'd barely pulled the curtains before reaching for the bottom of my shirt and tugging it over my head, and we were both naked and on top of the comforter a moment later.

The thing was, I'd been desperate to feel him next to me again, to run my hands over his skin and through his hair, to taste his tongue and the salty tang of sweat on his chest, to feel his heart beating against mine as he moved inside me. I'd been crushed to find out that Jane's Marty was coming to town, because all I had been able to picture since talking to Michael on the phone was the two of us naked and in my bed, for hours, if not days.

But Michael's eagerness outstripped mine. If

I hadn't known him so well, inside and out, I might have been a little frightened. I was definitely startled at first, because Michael was typically the epitome of a slow, purposeful lover. Unless we were really pressed for time or both exhausted, he liked to linger, kissing and caressing and teasing, stretching out foreplay until we were both crazy to have him inside me.

Not that day. He was hard and ready before I'd even processed the fact that he was kissing me so roughly my teeth had knocked together and my mouth felt bruised. And then he was thrusting inside me, so forcefully that I gasped.

When I came, it was shattering, that sudden, tightly wound coil of arousal springing with a kind of violence. I was panting, sweating, breathless—and certain that this unexpected caveman routine was due to the long months we'd been apart. I wasn't really surprised, once I thought about it, and we lay together afterward as we always did, this time on top of the bed-clothes, our heart rates slowing and the hungry flame of sex fading to a warm, comfortable glow.

When he joined me in the shower and took me up against the slippery white tile wall only an hour later, with the hot spray of water pounding on his back, I was startled all over again. But I was also startled by my own arousal. That hunger was a good thing, too, because for the remainder of that weekend, I think we left the room maybe twice, and ate only once more often.

He couldn't stop touching me, and he touched me in ways he never had. We did things we never had before, and most of it without speaking. I had expected to spend most of our time together talking—Michael was the word-smith, the one who needed to explicate every emotion and situation with language, and after the months we'd been separated, I had been prepared to recount almost every moment for him. But while I couldn't say he didn't care what had changed my mind about our relation-ship, or how I had spent the time without him, clearly the more important thing to him that weekend was marking me as his.

It felt that way, at least, and I was a little ashamed at what a turn-on it was. He was the same Michael, with his dark, watchful eyes, and his easy, loping grace, his hair a bit longer than when I'd seen him last, his frame thinner, but he was different in a fundamental way. He didn't ask me before spreading my legs, didn't try to seduce me, didn't prepare me for his entry. He took what he wanted, pure and simple, and it didn't matter—I was ready for him every time, wet and flushed and hungry. That he wanted me still, after I'd pushed him away, and that he wanted me with such intensity, was intoxicating.

Only once did he make me cry. Not in physical pain—no matter how aggressive he was, I knew he wouldn't hurt me, and he didn't—but because of what he'd asked.

It was late on Saturday night. We'd made love what seemed like dozens of times that day already, and twice since we'd come back from the restaurant where we'd eaten dinner. Our clothes were strewn around the room, and the dresser and night table were littered with soda cans and the crumpled wrappers from a couple of Hershey bars we'd picked up at the deli on the corner. The air was thick with the smell of our lovemaking, layered over the dusty drapes and the musty aroma of the hunter green carpet, and the sheets were a tangled, damp mess.

He'd stretched me out on the mattress, naked and still boneless from our last go-round. The only reality was his hands, his mouth, his wet, warm tongue, and I was trembling by the time he slid inside me, moving in lazy, agonizing thrusts. My fingers dug into his waist as I urged him deeper, faster, but instead, he pulled nearly all the way out of me, kissing my eyes shut, and whispered, "Say my name, Tess. Say my name."

When I replied, his name emerged on the heels of a sob, a ragged sound that only the two of us would recognize as the word *Michael*. I couldn't make sense of my reaction at the time, but it didn't matter. He heard me, and as he slid inside me again, he licked the tears off my cheeks.

Later I understood what had struck me so forcefully, and as Michael slept beside me on the sagging motel mattress, his eyes darting back and forth in a dream beneath his closed lids, I wept a few more frightened, helpless tears. He wanted to be the only man I ever saw—in my life, in my imagination, maybe in my own dreams—and he wasn't going to ask if he wasn't. I had nearly let him go, this man who loved me so wholly, so intensely, and the solid, tangible fact of him beside me in that bed was such a relief I couldn't help crying again.

It never occurred to me that the vehemence of Michael's lovemaking that weekend had anything to do with guilt. As far as I knew, the guilty party was, and always would be, me.

CHAPTER SEVENTEEN

IT WAS HARD TO COOK A DECENT meal with two teenagers making eyes at each other in the same room. It was even harder to concentrate when my husband was right there, too, slouched against the counter in jeans and a loose blue oxford I had always loved on him. Every time I looked at him—every time he looked at *me* with that lusty glimmer of awareness in his eyes—I was taken right back to last night.

After I'd cried myself out, Michael hadn't even bothered to get me into bed. Right there on the rug, which smelled faintly of dog and needed to be vacuumed, he'd lain me down and made love to me with his hands, his mouth, exploring me as if it was the first time, until I was nearly boneless with sensation.

But when he was about to come inside me, I managed to wriggle upright and push him onto his back. I wanted—no, needed—to make love to him that night. To communicate in every possible way that I was choosing to love him, that I had made my choice long ago and never once regretted it. And as I straddled him there on the floor, panting down at him as he stared at me, eyes glittering with pleasure, the release washed us clean.

Not that I should think about that now, I reminded myself as I gently smacked Michael's hand away from my waist. Jesse and Emma were holding hands across the kitchen table, their blond heads nearly the same color. Jesse's hair was spiked in the relentlessly casual way boys seemed to have learned in the past few years, and a tiny silver hoop I hadn't noticed on prom night glistened in one earlobe.

He had a man's hands already, I noticed as he took a tortilla chip from the bowl Emma had set out with salsa. They were big, strong hands, and already a bit rough, as if he'd used them for much more than text messaging and Xbox games. They were capable. Of far too many grown-up things.

I didn't know what to make of that, or if I was overreacting. I was so tired it was difficult to remember what I had to do next to get dinner on the table.

Michael and I had stayed up much too late once we'd finally collected ourselves and climbed into bed. It had felt so good to talk, the words poured out of us in streams; each wave flowing into the next. I told him about the gallery show Alicia had invited me to participate in; he told me what Drew had looked like in the hospital bed in Boston and how scared he had been to explain that first phone call all those weeks ago. I described the dresses Nell and I had chosen for her wedding, and he told me, when I asked, that Sophia believed her diaphragm had failed—how she'd gotten pregnant had been a niggling question in the back of my mind for weeks—

"Mom, can I help?" Emma asked, breaking my reverie. The question sounded guileless, but I could tell Jesse was impressed. At least she was showing off with an offer of assistance, instead of the bored teenage eye rolling I had expected.

"Sure, honey." I pointed to the water boiling on the stove. "You can get the pasta going."

Michael took her place at the table, lounging back in his chair comfortably as Emma bustled around the stove. "So, Jesse, Emma tells me you're in a band."

"Yes, sir." The boy immediately flushed with pleasure, or possibly embarrassment, I thought, that Emma had told her father about his musical aspirations. "I play the guitar, and I sing a little."

"Really?" Michael's eyebrows lifted. "I know a little about the guitar."

I hid a smile by ducking into the fridge for the Parmesan. My husband, the imaginary heir to Stevie Ray Vaughan. He played about as well as he danced ballet, but I had never had the heart to tell him that. I simply stashed his old acoustic in the attic whenever I could.

Emma and I left them to discuss garage rock versus the new alternative bands while we finished preparing the meal. The herb bread emerged from the oven golden brown, and I'd outdone myself with the sauce this time around—the kitchen smelled heavenly. Emma finished putting together a green salad, and then it was time to eat—she had cleaned up the dining room and set the table earlier, although I'd drawn the line at using the good china.

Was this the way my mother had felt when I started bringing Michael home? Apprehensive, nostalgic, a bit sad? Nothing said childhood was ending the way a teenager with a boyfriend did, after all. But as we sat down and dug in, I had to admit that Jesse was well-mannered and bright enough. The fact that he was smitten with Emma was almost painfully obvious.

We talked about the school play, set to premiere in just a few days, and about Jesse's plans for the summer, which I was pleased to hear included a part-time job at the supermarket. The conversation circled around the table lazily, and I let myself sit back and relax as Michael cleared the plates to make room for the buttery pound cake I'd made for dessert.

He was just walking back into the dining room when Emma piped up, "How's Drew doing, Dad? Any news?" Her tone was guileless, but she'd let her hair fall forward to curtain her eyes.

I choked back a spurt of fury. *Not the time, Emma.* Poor Jesse wouldn't look at any of us— his gaze was firmly fixed on the window over the backyard, and his cheeks had pinked up. The name didn't seem to be a surprise to him, but talking about Drew probably wasn't what he'd had in mind. What was Emma thinking?

Michael was still trying to formulate an answer to Emma's original question when she spoke up again. "Any word on blood marrow donors?" She was making room for the dessert plates as if we were simply continuing the earlier conversation, and doing a good job of appearing perfectly innocent. Frozen in my chair, the silence ringing around us, I wanted to strangle her.

"I haven't spoken to him today," Michael told her as he sat down. His expression was careful, and I reached for his hand across the table. "I don't think there's any news. As far as I know they haven't discharged him from the hospital yet."

Emma nodded, and I started to slice the pound cake. I couldn't guess where she was going with this, and I wasn't sure I wanted to. We'd had a pleasant dinner. *Don't ruin it,* I pleaded silently as I handed plates across to her and Jesse.

Michael opened his mouth to say something—to change the subject, I was sure—but Emma beat him to it.

"I was thinking about the whole transplant thing," she said, and I swallowed hard. With dusk gathering outside and the gentle fragrance of the first roses blooming in the air, the dining room was a peaceful oasis from all the stress and confusion of the past few weeks. And Emma seemed determined to ignore it, and to ignore the boy beside her, who was more uncomfortable every moment.

"There are only a few other options," Michael said slowly, his fork poised over his plate. "Since I'm not a match and neither is his mom."

"But I might be."

My heart plummeted into my stomach, and I managed one wild glance at Michael before Emma continued. That she had proposed this on her own made me both terrified and incredibly proud. She was growing up, no denying it.

"I've been researching donor matching on the Internet," she said calmly, reaching for the warm chocolate sauce to pour over her pound cake. "Parents only match one percent of the time, but siblings have a twenty-five percent chance of matching. I want to be tested. I want to see if I'm a match, so I can help him."

Through the haze of shock, I suddenly understood. She'd asked to have Jesse to dinner for just this reason. With him as witness, Michael and I were forced to be polite, to listen to her argument—at least for now. There would be no embarrassing scene in front of this boy, and she knew it.

Our daughter was pretty damn smart. She'd figured out on her own something Michael and Sophia had only recently discussed with Drew's doctors, and she'd picked the moment to propose her plan with the cool accuracy of a trial attorney.

"You said it yourself," she told Michael, her eyes as bright and clear as a spring day. "He's dying. Anything we can do to help him, we have to do. You were tested, Daddy. I should be, too."

What a change—the child who had freaked out at the idea of a half brother had come around completely. But the sad part was that I couldn't decide if she would have accepted Drew so easily if he hadn't been ill. Maybe everything did happen for a reason, whether we made choices or not. Maybe the choices we made told more about us than I'd ever realized.

"Emma, siblings may have a one in four chance of matching," I said, amazed that my voice didn't shake, "but you know that as a half sibling your chances will probably be cut in half, don't you?"

"Twelve and a half percent is still a lot more than one percent," Jesse said quietly, surprising us all. Obviously he and Emma had spent some time discussing this.

Emma was quick to jump back in. "There was a case in Illinois a few years ago where the half siblings matched but the father didn't," she argued. "It's not impossible. And it's worth trying. What if I am a match? Would you really want me to just sit back and let him die?"

"Of course not," I said, then blinked. Had I said that? Did I mean it? I was relieved to realize that I did, and as Michael stared across the table at me, I saw tears glistening in his eyes.

"You do know what the matching process requires, don't you?" he asked Emma when he'd collected himself. "What donating can mean if you match?"

She nodded, and if I thought she looked a bit paler than she had a moment earlier, I didn't blame her. The initial testing process wasn't difficult, but donating marrow could mean extracting it from her pelvic bones. The idea made me shudder, and I had to fight the gut instinct of keeping my child far from any unnecessary pain.

"I can do it, Dad," she said. Jesse was holding her hand. He was a little pale himself, but I couldn't miss the admiration that seemed to glow from inside him. I also didn't miss the fact that he had reached for her, instead of the other way around.

"You know what?" Michael stood up without warning and ran his hands through his hair, a tentative smile on his lips. "Why don't you two finish your dessert and then load the dishwasher while your mom and I take Walter for a walk."

"Um, okay." Emma sounded confused, but I didn't stop to reassure her. Michael had already called the dog and headed into the kitchen to find his leash.

"We'll be back in twenty minutes," I said as my husband led me out the door and down the front steps.

Out on the walk, Michael put his arm around me, and I twisted sideways to glance at him in the twilight. "What is this all about?"

"I needed air," he said, pulling me closer as we turned onto the sidewalk. It was just another weeknight on the block—lights had just begun to burn in the windows, fireflies flickered above the lawns and the tang of citronella on backyard decks was sharp in the air. The quiet felt wrong, given the bomb Emma had dropped. "I don't know about you, but I never thought I could be so damn proud of Emma and so terrified of her at the same time. And I wasn't about to lose it in front of the teenage Romeo in there."

"Terrified *of* her?" Walter tugged on the leash to edge closer to a clump of dandelions, his tail wagging furiously.

"I'm scared for her, too," Michael admitted as we paused to let Walter do his business along the curb. "Pain isn't fun, and there are always risks to the donor. But yeah, I'm more terrified of her. She's only fifteen, babe, and right now I'm a little amazed at how strong-willed she's become. Not to mention how grown-up. I guess I'm glad she's on our side. She planned that ambush pretty well, don't you think?"

"Pretty well?" I laid my head against his shoulder. "I'll be surprised if the military doesn't draft her into its strategy department."

He was right, though. An Emma with her mind made up, and rational reasons for making it up the way she had, was much scarier than the incoherent bundle of emotion she had been for the past few weeks.

Even so, I understood how love could carry you away, how you could find yourself somewhere you never expected to be. And I was beginning to understand that all kinds of love could do that, not just the first glimmer of attraction for a crush, as fresh and bright as a firefly, or the hot, steady flames of passion that had burned for longer than you could remember.

I didn't think Emma loved Drew yet, not really, but she loved the idea of family, of a brother, and especially the notion of being adult enough to change the world.

And saving a life did that. If Drew died instead of lived, untold things would never happen. Some people would never laugh, or never love, or never be born. And if Drew lived instead of died, the number of things that could happen because of him was endless.

Tears burned as I tugged on Walter's leash and let Michael turn us toward home in the warm dusk, grateful for his arm around my waist, and even more grateful that we were in synch again. Last night, he'd filled the windy hollowness inside me. I could only hope he felt the comfortable, familiar weight of my love the way I did his.

"Do you remember when she fell?" Michael asked me as we mounted the front steps. He bent to let Walter off the leash, and took my hand to lead me to the porch swing. It creaked as we sat down, and I kicked off my sandals to set it going with my toes against the gritty floor. Through the open window I heard Emma and Jesse at the dining-room table, laughing as they argued over something I couldn't make out.

"Of course I do," I told Michael, settling against him. "I've never been so scared in my life."

She had just turned four, and we'd moved into the house only a few months earlier—it was still mostly empty, the old floors devoid of carpets and the walls still in need of spackle and paint. For Emma, of course, it was a giant playroom, miles more spacious than the little rented Cape Cod where she had been born.

She and Michael had been playing hide-and-seek after dinner, which involved more running and giggly shrieks than I thought was strictly necessary, but I didn't really care. I'd been in the kitchen, finishing up the dishes—those were the bad old predishwasher days—and singing along to Hootie and the Blowfish on the radio, when I heard a horrible thumping sound that went on far too long, and a stunned silence that also seemed to stretch out interminably until I heard Emma gasp.

Michael's footsteps hammered down the steps as I dropped the glass I'd been drying and skidded into the front hall, only to find Emma crumpled at the bottom of the stairs.

"Oh my God. Oh God, is she breathing? Oh God. Oh God…"

I waved Michael away as I knelt beside her. She was clearly breathing—she was trying to catch her breath, in fact, she'd begun to sob so hard. It was the outraged pain and terror of a child shocked to find herself hurting, and my heart crashed in my chest as I scooped her into my arms. She was sweaty and overheated, a bundle of twiggy little bones, and I rocked her and shushed her as long as I could before I finally set her away from me, just far enough to look at her. She was still crying, shuddering with sobs.

"Oh God," Michael said again. The blood had drained from his face, and I was pretty sure that he would begin to tremble any minute. A nasty pink goose egg was already forming on Emma's forehead—she must have landed right on it, or bumped it hard as she tumbled down the stairs.

And despite my arms around her, despite my ceaseless murmur against her ear, she was still crying.

"She might have lost consciousness," I said to Michael. Everything felt strangely remote, even Michael's panic—the only thing I could focus on was Emma, shaking and choking on her sobs in my lap. "It took her a long time to cry out."

"Lost…?" He sat down heavily on the bottom step, and without thinking, I reached out and smacked his arm.

"Keep it together," I said in a fierce whisper. "We have to take her to the emergency room. Go up and get her blanket and her bunny. I'm going to put her in the car. Can you drive so I can sit in the back with her?"

He blinked once and then nodded and sprinted upstairs. I heaved her into my arms and grabbed a paper towel and a bag of frozen peas for her head before I bundled her into the car.

Emma had stopped crying only long enough to throw up all over her Elmo T-shirt and the backseat, and by the time we got to the E.R., the world had gone completely surreal for me. If the doctors didn't examine my daughter right away, I was oddly, calmly sure that I would begin to scream, possibly throw things, and threaten a kind of violence I had never known lurked inside me.

But they did see her immediately, and three hours later, as Michael and I drove home with

Emma asleep in the back seat, he reached forward to lay his hand on my shoulder. "I thought I broke her." His voice was a husky whisper. "I…I mean, we were just playing, like always, and I didn't think about her socks on the floor…"

I'd pulled over, parked beneath an ancient oak just blocks from our house and ran around the car to the back seat, where he had been sitting beside Emma. We held each other beneath a pale, watchful moon while he cried.

As we sat in the gently rocking swing now, he murmured, "I thought I broke her this time, too, you know? That finding out about Drew would shatter her—her ideas about us, her faith in us, her sense of security."

I nodded against his shoulder, but before I could say anything, he went on. "I always knew you would be all right."

There it was again, those innocent words that had hurt so much the first time. *You would be all right.* I hated to break the peace of the moment, but I had to ask. I pushed away. "Why? Do you know how much I love you, really? How could you believe I would be okay?"

Surprise rippled across his face. "Oh, babe, no. I didn't mean that you wouldn't care, that it wouldn't hurt, but that you would make it okay," he said. "That you would find a way to help me, to know what to do. Remember what I said about choice? I knew you would choose to believe in us, because I know exactly how much you love me."

I was crying again, the tears hot and wet against his shirt. I was ready for the time of tears to be over, but I was grateful for these—even more than last night, they were made of relief, a fabulous lightness that was like the first breath drawn after you'd been under water.

"She's not broken," Michael whispered as he held me. "And neither are we."

I nodded up at him, and wiped my cheeks with the back of my hand as he added, "Let's go tell her we're heading back to Cambridge."

CHAPTER EIGHTEEN

"I CAN'T DECIDE WHICH I'M MORE nervous about," Michael's mom, Maureen Butterfield, said quietly as we walked into Brigham and Women's Hospital nearly a week later. "Meeting Drew for the first time or Emma's testing."

I didn't blame her, and I took her hand to give it a warm squeeze as Michael held the door for us. Emma was already up ahead, carefully scanning the bustling lobby, wearing her hastily mustered confidence like armor.

Agreeing to let Emma undergo testing as a possible bone marrow match didn't mean anything would happen overnight, though. First there had been a flurry of phone calls back and forth to Sophia and Drew, between Sophia and the doctors and then back to us, appointments to schedule and travel arrangements to make, all with Emma's last week of school to consider.

Of course, after I'd seen the stunned amazement on her face when Michael and I told her we were proud of her and we would allow her to be tested, I would have walked all the way to Boston with Emma riding piggyback.

Still, doctors didn't tend to schedule testing on Saturdays, which meant more time off from work for Michael, and a desperate call to the high-school principal to reschedule an exam for Emma. I'd juggled appointments, too, but we couldn't leave until Sunday morning, since I had another wedding to photograph Saturday afternoon. I couldn't break a professional commitment—not at the last minute, at least—although concentrating on thrown bouquets and the right light for shots of the cake wasn't easy. Maureen had asked if she could come for dinner or, better yet, bring dinner, and neither Michael nor I had the heart to say no.

Maureen was, as always, the calm eye at the center of any storm. She'd been a practicing psychologist for more than forty years, a fact that had intimidated me when Michael and I first started dating. Would she know what I was thinking? Would she know what I was thinking when Michael had his arm around me? Did she know what we were doing when we were alone?

Silly teenage fears, of course, but I'd discovered over the years what Maureen had probably learned early on—being a good listener was the first step in being a good therapist. She had her boisterous moments, like anyone else, but for the most part she sat back and listened, and observed. As much as she enjoyed helping a patient work through a problem, she was fascinated by human behavior. She watched people the way some of us watched TV.

Naturally, she had understood a lot more about our long-ago separation than I had guessed at the time. What was more, she didn't blame either of us for it or for its consequences.

"Blame is useless," she'd told me one day not long after that horrible scene at my mother's table, when she'd shown up at the door with an armful of lilacs that had bloomed early. "What you need to deal with is facts, consequences. After a certain point it doesn't matter why someone did something. What matters is what you do about it now."

I'd gotten lucky where mothers-in-law were concerned, that was for sure. But I was so distracted by the thought of packing for the trip, of what would happen to Emma during the testing, that the idea of having Maureen over for dinner—even if she was bringing the meal— had made me a little cranky.

"I'm not sure what she's thinking," Michael had admitted that morning as I prepared for the wedding. "But she never does this kind of thing. I don't want to say no to her."

I didn't, either, not really. Maureen *wasn't* intrusive, or nosy, or needy. In fact, sometimes she was so low-key I forgot about her for a day or two, just across town in the house that had been too big even when Michael and Melissa had shared it with her. She'd never married again—she'd never even made a serious attempt at dating after Michael's dad died, which I thought was a shame. She was a lovely woman, gentle and reserved on first glance, with intelligence and a sly sense of humor that was sharper than you expected underneath.

And feelings Michael and I hadn't really considered. As she explained to us Saturday night over Chinese food, she wanted to meet her grandson.

Michael nearly swallowed part of his egg roll wrong, but I could see that he was appalled we hadn't considered this possibility, not that she wanted to do it.

"God, Mom, I'm so sorry, I just hadn't thought…" he began.

"Me, neither." I offered a helpless shrug. "I could make excuses, but there really are none."

"There's no need," Maureen said firmly. She helped herself to more beef with broccoli, then added a generous spoonful of the dark, pungent sauce before mixing the whole thing into her rice. She took a bite. "The two of you have had plenty on your minds without worrying about me."

With that she gave Emma a pointed look, and Emma at least had the decency to blush.

We were all quiet for a moment, except for Walter, who was whining at Michael's feet for a taste of our dinner. "Why don't you come with us, Gram," Emma said suddenly. She was pleased with herself, the same bright hopefulness in her eyes I had seen the other night. It made her appear both older and younger at the same time—clever, determined, but so idealistic. "You could drive up with us and meet Drew on Monday."

Was she aware that there might be only a few chances left for Maureen to meet this boy who was her grandson? I wasn't about to ask her, but judging by the glance that passed between Michael and his mother at the moment, they certainly understood it.

So we all climbed into the car Sunday morning, with a bagful of doughnuts from the bakery downtown and headed north again. This time, at least, Emma wasn't pouting, and Maureen had plenty of fond stories to share about her favorite patient, a man she referred to only as K., who had been in therapy for years and still couldn't get through a day without either calling her or developing a new phobia.

Now that we were in the hospital, though, I knew exactly what I was nervous about, and it was Emma. Between my knee surgery and the chaos of Emma's birth, my own experiences with the medical profession had been pretty unpleasant, and I was usually more than happy to keep my distance from any building with white-coated professionals inside. And here I was offering up my daughter, whose experience with pain so far had been nothing more than a skinned knee or a scraped elbow—aside from the concussion she didn't remember—for tests that would have turned my legs to jelly.

Drew and Sophia had planned to meet us upstairs in one of the family waiting rooms, and as we stepped onto the elevator, I felt Maureen fidgeting beside me. She was patting her hair into place, checking that her earrings were securely fastened, and I leaned over to kiss her cheek. "You look fine," I whispered.

She flushed with embarrassment, but just as the bell dinged for our floor she murmured, "You usually meet your grandchildren when they're too little to notice anything but a kind voice and a soft touch. This is a bit intimidating."

"He's cool, Gram," Emma said as she stepped off the elevator. "Really cool. He'll love you."

Michael slung his arm around Emma's shoulder. "Cool, Mom. Just keep that in mind."

"He thinks he's so amusing," Maureen muttered, but once we'd checked in with the nurse, she let me hold her hand. Michael knocked lightly on the door of the room Sophia and Drew were waiting in.

It was nothing special, even as hospital decor goes—colorless furniture against faintly tan walls, a fake spider plant hung clumsily in the grimy window that overlooked the street and tattered magazines already months old. But there was Drew, a book in his lap as he slouched on one of the sofas. His face lit up when we walked in, and before anyone said a word, he held out his arms and Emma dropped to the sofa beside him, hugging him hard.

Sophia bit her bottom lip—she was trying not to cry, I knew. Her eyes were glassy, and her cheeks were hot with emotion. I squeezed her hand when she approached us, but I let Michael introduce her to his mother. After dropping my bag on a table strewn with bone marrow literature and pieces of the *Boston Globe,* I fished out my trusty everyday camera, a digital I'd bought six months earlier.

I'd packed it at the last minute, and I wasn't sure why I dropped it into my handbag this morning—a hospital waiting room wasn't exactly the most scenic setting for photos. But the moment it was in my hand, I understood—this was my way to escape, just a little. When you're behind the lens, no one pays much attention to you, and the air in the room was nearly electric with awkwardness.

I was an old-school photographer—I kept the digital for snapshots, studies for future shoots, parties and birthdays. Film was my true medium because I could play with exposures, lighting, cropping and all kinds of effects when I developed it. The digital didn't offer a lot of choices for light, and there would be no way to disguise the surroundings—at least, not until I could PhotoShop it—but the picture Drew and Emma made together needed to be captured.

I heard Maureen's and Sophia's soft voices as they talked, but I couldn't see anything except my daughter and her half brother. Emma's blond head had dropped onto Drew's shoulder, and his arm was curled protectively around her. Whatever they'd talked about in all those e-mails had clearly made them siblings in ways I never would have expected, and for the first time I could notice a resemblance between them. The angle of Michael's jaw was there in each face; their father was in the shape of their eyes, a softness in their mouths.

I took the first shot just as Emma turned her face up to Drew's, something he'd said twisting her mouth into a grin. They glanced up when the flash went off, mirror images of surprise, and I took another shot. Then another, as they began to mug for me, heads touching, making faces, laughing.

Just like a brother and sister.

I realized that the room had gone quiet behind me, and I spun around without warning to take a shot of Michael, Maureen and Sophia, watching the kids, all their love and fear evident on their faces.

Maureen rolled her eyes—she hated herself in photos, even if she claimed I did a better job than anyone at making her look "not completely horrific," as she put it.

"Stop it, you," I told her with a smirk. "Or I'll take even more."

She waved a hand and moved out of the way, and I pointed the lens at Michael and Sophia. They stood just inches apart, observing the interplay with interest, similar in height, both of them dark and lean, and I snapped them that way before suggesting, "Get closer, guys. Arms around each other, maybe. Come on. Pretend you like each other."

That startled laughter out of Drew and Emma, but Sophia and Michael did as I asked, and they were comfortable together in the shot. Like parents. It took me aback for a moment.

This was family, I thought, putting my camera aside as a ripple of awareness swept through me. No matter how new it was, how unfamiliar, we were family, disparate, fragile strands woven into one cord. There was no way to judge how strong it was.

"Drew." Michael walked across to the sofa as Drew stood, and the two of them hugged, the brief, hard embrace of men. "I want you to meet my mom, Maureen Butterfield."

Beside Sophia, in her skinny faded jeans and a loose white blouse, her dark hair a careless pile of curls on top of her head, Maureen was as polished and stiff as a silver teapot. She'd let her dark hair go gray years ago, and it was a gorgeous pewter. She was terribly nervous—her face was set too carefully, her hands stiff at her sides. She'd taken longer than usual to dress at the hotel this morning, and I knew she wasn't happy with the plain khaki slacks and navy blue shirt she'd chosen. I'd never seen her so unsure of herself.

If Drew felt the same way, he certainly didn't show it. It was impossible to miss how much thinner he'd gotten in just a few weeks, but there was color in his cheeks, and he opened his arms to Maureen easily.

"I'm, uh, Drew," he said after a minute, and everyone laughed.

"Maureen Butterfield," Maureen said with a little smile. Just like that, the tension had melted away, and her rigid shoulders relaxed. "I imagine you're a bit too old to call me Gram, but I'd be happy for you to call me Maureen."

"I think I can handle that." He kissed her cheek lightly, and she gave his hand a squeeze just as the nurse from the reception desk peeked inside.

"We're ready for Emma," she said, checking her clipboard. Brisk efficiency with a friendly layer of warmth—the best kind of nurse, in my opinion. "Emma?"

I took a deep breath as my daughter got up. The urge to hold her back was nearly irresistible, but when I moved to hug her before she left the room, she stopped me with a shake of her head.

"I'll be fine, Mom," she said, and then glanced at Drew. There were whole worlds of wisdom and faith in her eyes. "We'll be fine."

As she walked away, I found it was impossible not to believe her.

CHAPTER NINETEEN

I HAD A LOT OF TIME TO THINK about my daughter in the weeks between that initial cheek swab and the actual process of her donating her bone marrow. She'd taught me something about love and choices with her insistence on getting tested, but sometimes I believed I'd been learning from her since the moment she was born.

I spent six full days in the hospital after Emma arrived. An emergency C-section and a surprise hysterectomy will do that to you, of course. Emma was fine—almost eight pounds, pink and round and furiously hungry every moment she was awake, despite her impromptu entry into the world—but my OB arranged to keep her in with me until I was ready to be discharged. If they'd sent her home without me, I probably would have followed after Michael in my hospital gown, stitches still screaming and my feet jammed into slippers.

Those days in the hospital were a blur, a

vague impression of pain and exhaustion, coupled with the fiercest love I had ever known. Emma was little more than a strangely demanding mouth at that point, a foreign creature that nevertheless smelled intoxicatingly good. A foreign creature, but mine to care for, and I loathed letting her go even for diaper changes. Whatever apprehension I'd felt when I'd realized I was pregnant had faded into nothingness when I gazed at her face for the first time. I fell asleep nursing her most afternoons, my head bent forward to breathe in that clean, innocent scent from her peach-fuzz skull.

Recuperating from major surgery is rough even when you don't have a newborn to care for, and when Michael was finally allowed to take us home, I was so grateful to him I burst into tears more than once the first day. Hormones, my mother said, but I knew it was more. I relied on him for almost everything, and it had never occurred to me that there were women whose husbands would have willingly cleaned a gas station toilet before changing a newborn's diaper or helping his still-bleeding wife into the bathroom for an emergency sanitary pad.

And beyond that—in those first days, my gratitude was so huge I could barely see over the top of it—there was the way Michael had fallen in love with Emma. He was every kind of adorable, heartbreaking fool, cooing to her, watching her as she slept, fascinated as her miniature fingers tightened around his thumb.

What amazed me from time to time, as I stared blearily into the darkened bedroom during a 3:00 a.m. feeding, was how one tiny person changed everything. Before, we were two people, in love with each other, committed to making a life together, but that didn't really require much more than agreeing on which sofa to buy, or what to watch on TV in the evening, or what to have for dinner. We had separate interests, separate careers; we saw friends on our own as often as we went out together.

Of course, the key was that we got to come home to the nest we'd made together and find each other there. Every evening was reassuringly familiar—we'd change out of our work clothes, idly discuss ordinary household chores like the laundry and the grocery shopping. Michael would read as I did yoga or sorted through photos, or we'd pass pieces of the paper back and forth as we lay on the bed with the TV on in the background. Some nights Michael tapped away at his first novel while I rustled up dinner and sang along to the radio.

It was an easy, comfortable existence, exactly what we'd expected when we'd gotten married. Yes, we had to pay the rent and the bills and keep ourselves in food and clothes, but we managed it pretty handily. Our most pressing decisions usually revolved around whether to troop over to Murray's Bagels on a Sunday morning, or stay home and make pancakes.

And yet here we were with a baby. Michael and I had made a whole new human being, for heaven's sake. A person we were entirely responsible for, every moment of her life, at least until she was an adult. I stared into her little pink face all the time, in wonder, as she pursed her mouth or flailed one arm that had escaped from her blanket. I was pretty sure it would be nearly impossible to feel that she wasn't "ours" even when she was off working at a career, getting married and maybe raising her own children.

That fierce love was nothing every new parent hasn't felt, but it was my first maternal revelation, and therefore brand new as well as stunning. As I sat propped in bed one day with Emma in my arms, warm and milky and entirely, incredibly perfect in every way, it dawned on me that what Michael and I were used to was finding our love mirrored in each other's eyes. We never had to look farther than each other to see the person who meant more to us than anyone else. Now we had an outside focus, this tiny interloper who loomed so huge in our lives, a child we would care for together, a child who would force us to look away from each other once in a while, but who would bring us closer together than ever.

"Where's my girl? Let me hold her," he'd say as soon as he walked into the apartment after work. I was usually happy to let him after a long day of one-on-one time with Emma, who had her cranky moments just like any brand-new person adjusting to a world that must have seemed enormous and cold after all those cozy months in the womb.

But soon enough Emma would begin the panicky mewl that meant she was hungry, and my breasts would begin to leak, and Michael would moan that he wanted to give her a bottle. We were both a bit like kids fighting over a favorite toy.

One day was particularly bad. It had rained since noon, squashing the walk Emma and I usually took through the Village, and she had been restless and whimpery for hours. To top it off, she'd been up nearly all night, or so it seemed, and I was so tired I could have whimpered a little bit myself.

Our one-bedroom apartment was small and arranged railroad style, with a hallway connecting the adjoined living room and kitchen, the bathroom and our bedroom. The living room was crowded with books and camera equipment and Michael's desk, as well as the swing my parents had given us for Emma, and the bedroom was a nightmare of dirty laundry, Emma's bassinet and our bed crowded into a room that was barely big enough to fit our shared dresser. None of it even registered as I plodded up and down that hallway, patting the baby's back, for more than an hour. Her frustrated cranking turned into an official screech about twenty minutes before Michael walked in, and I thrust her at him before bursting into tears.

"She won't stop," I managed to get out between sniffling sobs as I collapsed on the sofa, "and she won't eat, and she's not wet, and I'm so tired, Michael, I mean, so tired…"

To give him credit, he didn't even crack a smile. He shushed me while he shushed her, until I was at least a little calmer.

And then he got up, still in his tie and his work shoes, which he normally kicked off the moment he was inside, and started a circuit of our tiny living room with Emma propped against his shoulder. He looped around the coffee table, stopped at the bookcase to show her his favorite novels, paused at the window to give her a view of Sixth Avenue.

She was still muttering, squirming and screwing up her face the way she did when she was working up to a full-fledged scream. That was when Michael started to sing. To the tune of "Old McDonald's Farm," he ad-libbed his way around the living room again as he stroked her back. "Your poor mommy is so tired. Yes, she really is. And when she's tired, she cries, too. Yes, she really does…."

As if by magic, Emma turned toward the sound of his voice, her huge eyes still that dark, newborn blue, and sighed. After another two choruses, her lids began to droop, until she was finally, miraculously, asleep.

Somewhere in the back of my mind, I was furious that Michael had been able to soothe her when I couldn't, but I knew that even so, I had just fallen in love with him a bit harder. The image of him walking around that small room, his favorite blue-striped tie crushed between his chest and Emma's compact little body, was something I would never forget.

Even now, it seemed, our little girl wanted her daddy for comfort.

It was late June, and Emma had just been

wheeled out of the recovery room after the marrow extraction process. She'd been right— probably through sheer force of will, I thought secretly, with more than a little glow of pride— she was a match for Drew. Despite how desperately Drew needed her marrow, though, he had to undergo pretransplant protocol first, which involved intense chemo and radiation for a few weeks beforehand.

"Essentially, it will destroy his immune system," Sophia had explained when we heard the news that Emma was a perfect donor. "But that will keep his body from rejecting the cells. Even if they match, I guess the body knows they're invaders."

Invasion was a distressingly familiar concept even then—when the process of the bone marrow extraction had been explained by the transplant center doctors, I was impressed with the way Emma listened, calm and completely unruffled, at least on the surface. She was to be given general anesthesia, for one, then placed facedown as the doctors inserted large, hollow needles into her pelvic bones to extract the marrow. The thought made me vaguely nauseous.

But it was her body, as Michael reminded me when I paled and sat down abruptly. Dr. Bonfiglio was alarmed until I assured him I was simply surprised. I accepted a paper cup of water and nodded when Michael whispered, "Her choice."

I'd learned enough about choices in the past few weeks to realize how important it was that Emma have the chance to make some of her own.

Now Michael was seated on the edge of Emma's bed, telling her silly knock-knock jokes and doing bad imitations of the transplant staff. And, unbelievably, she was smiling. She was so pale it was a little frightening, and she didn't look quite awake yet. The skin under her eyes was smudged a faint blue-gray, and she kept swallowing, as if her mouth was dry, but there was no mistaking the gentle upward curve of her lips. I was trying my best to ignore the IV that snaked down from the metal pole beside the bed and into the back of her hand.

"Okay, the really skinny one, with the purple streak in her hair?" Michael said now. "She sounds like a bird on Valium, with that really weird squawk." He tried to approximate it and succeeded only in making himself sound sort of like a dying cow.

But Emma laughed, which was the point. "Daddy, you're a goof."

"Yes. Yes, I am." He pretended to hang his head, then winked at her.

I turned around when I heard a light rap on the door. It was Sophia, poking her head in tentatively. "Can I come in?"

"Please." I got up from the single visitor's chair, but she waved away my offer.

"I wanted to see how Emma did." She handed Emma a lush, hand-picked bouquet of daylilies. "I brought cookies, too," she said, pulling a container of chocolate chips out of her tote bag, "but I'm not sure if you're allowed to eat them yet."

"Let's find out," Emma said with a weak laugh. She pushed herself upright and winced. "I am kind of hungry now, and those look way better than a hospital meal."

Michael was up before I could make a move for the door. "I'll check."

I let Sophia and Emma chat for a few minutes and sank back in the torturous plastic chair. If I'd been able to smell the cookies through the plastic container, at least one of them would have been gone already. I hadn't eaten since breakfast, and between prep, anesthesia, the actual procedure and Emma's two hours in the recovery room, I was suddenly weak with hunger myself.

At least Sophia seemed interested only in Emma. For reasons I didn't really understand, my brief feeling of kinship with her had faded so completely I sometimes wondered if it had ever happened. Nothing had changed, but every time I glanced at her I found myself inexplicably angry.

My reaction had nothing to do with Drew or what Emma had undergone for him. The more I knew of Michael's son, the more I liked him. The same day Emma had been tested, while we all waited in the cafeteria, Drew had pulled a manila folder out of his backpack and handed it to me with a hopeful grin.

"Michael brought these to me when I was sick, and I wanted to tell you how much I loved them. You highlighted everything cool about architecture."

Inside, an old series of my photos was tied carefully with a piece of string. I'd taken them when we still lived in New York, shortly before we got married, as we'd wandered all over the city on weekend afternoons, scouting out interesting buildings and unusual angles from which to shoot them.

And Michael had shared them with his son, the architecture student. I was touched, both at Michael's gesture and Drew's genuine appreciation. He wasn't angling for a stepmother or even a stand-in aunt, which was fortunate, since I didn't really have an interest in playing either of those roles. But I was certain that over time we would be friends.

Sophia, on the other hand, was a different story. Maybe if I tried, if I dragged my feelings out into the light and examined them a little more closely, I could figure out what had changed my reaction to her, but today wasn't the day to do that. Not when I was too exhausted to think straight.

The door swung open, and Michael ambled in again, a smile on his face. "The powers that be say solid food is okay if you're up to it, babe," he told Emma, sitting on the side of the bed again. "Maybe I should try one first, though."

Emma snatched the cookie away with another laugh. "Good try, Dad."

"I know someone else who probably needs to eat." Sophia laid a hand on my shoulder. She was wearing some kind of light perfume, and it reminded me of freshly washed laundry, dried in the sun. "How about some lunch, my treat?"

Oh, God. What was I supposed to say? Michael and Emma had frozen, two pairs of brown eyes trained on me, waiting for my response. There was no way to refuse—at least, not politely.

"It'll have to be hospital food, but the chicken salad actually isn't half-bad." Sophia's tone was light, but I didn't miss the plea in it.

Oh, okay, I thought, trying not to grit my teeth. *One meal.*

"You don't mind?" I asked Emma as I stood up and gathered my bag. A last-ditch attempt, but worth a shot.

She shook her head, another cookie already in her mouth. "I'll be fine," she mumbled.

Michael very pointedly refused to look at me, the weasel, and pretended to be interested in choosing another cookie from the container. I was on my own.

We rode down to the cafeteria in silence, and it wasn't until we were in line—with the suggested chicken-salad sandwiches on our trays—that Sophia said, "I guess I just wanted to thank you, Tess. This is awkward, all of it, but what Emma's done is so huge for Drew. And for me. Waiting for another donor could have taken… Well, a really long time."

Too long. She didn't say it, but it was the truth. I let her pay for lunch when the cashier totaled up our purchases, and made my way to a table in the corner, overlooking the gift shop, before I answered her.

"You don't have to thank me," I said finally, when Sophia was seated across from me. "You don't really have to thank Emma, either. She wanted to do this, and in all truth, I don't think we could have stopped her. She knew exactly how important a possible match could be."

Her smile was rueful. "Some people might not offer, even so. And other people wouldn't let their teenage daughter offer."

Offer. There it was, without warning, the reason I found myself tempted to shake her, or shout at her. The infuriating splinter in the back of my mind that I had never been able to get to.

The words tumbled out before I thought twice.

"Why didn't you ask?" I realized my hands had clenched into fists when I felt my nails digging into my palms. "Your son was dying, Sophia. Why didn't you *ask* if we would get Emma tested?"

Shock left her mouth slack, and I felt the wave of anger off her as if an oven door had been opened. But I didn't care—that was it, that was what had been bothering me. That she hadn't suggested Emma might be able to help Drew when Michael couldn't, that she hadn't, in some remote part of my brain, done every last thing to save her child's life.

And in an even more distant, hateful part of my brain, I was worried that Michael would find her unwillingness to intrude on our lives, and our daughter's health, admirable.

It didn't really make sense, even to me. If

anything, Michael would stand up and noisily applaud any parent who lay down in traffic for his or her kid, damn the consequences. I could see it, though—Sophia the saint, who would never think of asking for anything for herself, or even her sick child. Sophia the selfless, who would never impinge on another's happiness or well-being—and therefore deserved help all the more. Apparently, most logic had fallen out of my brain sometime in the past two months.

I was actually a bit startled when Sophia simply took a deep breath and mustered up another rueful smile, instead of throwing her paper cup of diet ginger ale in my face. The woman had invited me to lunch, for heaven's sake, and my first gesture had been to attack her. Okay, maybe I did care. My cheeks burned with embarrassment, but I was still curious how she would answer me.

"I wanted to bring it up the night I called Michael the first time," she admitted. Her eyes had a faraway look, their dark depths trained on a spot across the bustling dining room. "When he told me about you and Emma. I wanted to beg him to come up the next day and bring Emma with him so they could both be tested. But Drew made me promise I wouldn't, at least not then, not when he didn't even know Michael or Emma. It wasn't easy, let me tell you. I was about ready to start jumping people on the street just to ask about their bone marrow."

I couldn't help it—I smiled at that.

"You know, Drew is a man now, even if he is still a young one," Sophia went on. She'd picked up her soda and was staring thoughtfully at the straw. "He'll always be my baby, same way Emma will always be yours, but that doesn't mean they don't eventually grow up, you know? And Drew has been very vocal from the start about the way he wanted to handle this. He's stubborn, my kid." She laughed a little as she lifted her gaze to mine. "It doesn't mean he's not angry about this, or that he hasn't done his share of ranting and throwing things at the wall, but he's always been in charge of this. His life, his death. That's what he said. He knows what he wants, always has."

He sounded more like Michael every minute, and for a moment I felt tears threatening. Drew deserved to know his dad. And he definitely deserved a chance to a life lived outside a hospital's walls.

"Don't get me wrong, either," Sophia added before I could say anything. "If you and Michael hadn't come to me about what Emma wanted to do, I would have asked, believe me,

Drew's rules be damned. He's all I have, and he has everything on earth ahead of him."

Afraid to speak right away, I simply nodded. There were all kinds of choices to make in the course of a life, and it was beginning to seem to me that the most important ones were completely unexpected.

I couldn't let this chance to raise one more question slip by, though. I took a sip of my iced tea and finally raised my face to hers. "Can I ask why you didn't tell Michael about Drew back when you found out you were pregnant?"

She shook her head with a curious laugh. "Tess, I told you that the day I called you. Michael and I...those months were wonderful. He's caring and kind and smart and unbelievably sexy, but I couldn't compete. He was with me, yeah, but he never stopped talking about you." She reached across the table and laid her hand over mine. "And I didn't want to be with a man who was so completely in love with another woman. That was my choice, Tess. It wasn't easy on Drew, which was selfish of me, but it was certainly a hell of a lot easier on my heart."

I had never known relief could be so palpable. I hadn't realized that a few small, stubborn doubts had lingered in my imagination and in my heart.

And I had never even considered that I could be grateful to this woman who had given my husband a son.

CHAPTER TWENTY

"AND NOW YOU MAY KISS the bride."

The minister, a kindly older man Nell had met at the hospital, offered the words with a smile, and Jack and Nell leaned into each other gratefully, hands clasped, for their first kiss as husband and wife.

It went on a bit longer than anyone antici-pated, and finally my brother Will, the youngest of us, began to clap. Matt followed with a hoot of joy, and Nell and Jack parted, flushed and grinning, to start down the aisle.

I had crept away from the makeshift altar, set up on the wide side porch of the Willowdale Farm house, when they exchanged rings. The shot of the kiss was from a distance, but I knew Nell would want more pictures of her and Jack as they came down the aisle arm in arm. To my surprise, she stopped when she reached where

I stood behind the last row of seats. She didn't plan to, I could tell—she sort of jerked to a halt at the last moment, the creamy satin of her skirt rustling. Jack was startled, but his grin widened as Nell leaned over and kissed my cheek. She was full to the brim with joy—it was bubbling over, and she was eager to share.

"Thank you," she whispered. Happy tears made her eyes sparkle in the late-afternoon sunlight slanting through the screens. "Thank you for giving me the courage to wait for the real thing."

And then she was gone, disappearing through the French doors into the side parlor of the old house with Jack. In another moment I heard them laughing with relief and celebration.

"She thanked me," I told Michael as we waited for cocktails at the bar a few minutes later, when he asked why Nell had paused. "She actually said I was the reason she 'waited for the real thing.'" Puzzled, I looked up at him, and he shook his head before he took his martini from the bartender.

"You don't think you deserve it?" he murmured, and put his arm around me. He was gorgeous in his dark suit, his hair newly cut and the faint scent of his aftershave a spicy warmth. "You don't think we do?"

A few months ago, it would have been a loaded question. Today, with my sister's wedding reception before us on a bright early-fall afternoon, I offered up a sheepish shrug in reply. He was right, as usual.

Some of Nell's happiness bubbled through me then, deliciously light. It was almost unbelievable to me that we were standing here, the summer behind us, and with it all of the pain and confusion that had begun with a simple phone call on a Tuesday evening in May.

The whole south side of the farmhouse had been opened into one large room, with the pocket doors between what had been the original dining room and parlor tucked away. And since I had last seen Willowdale Farm in May, the owners had completely refurbished the place. The wide-plank floors gleamed, fresh creamy paint adorned the woodwork and the reception room had been simply decorated with white ribbon, white tea roses, glossy green garlands and candles.

Across the room, silhouetted by the floor-to-ceiling window, Emma stood with Drew, and Sophia was nearby talking to one of Jack's friends. I didn't remember his name, but he was a research chemist with an incredibly dry sense of humor. He was also surprisingly sexy—

suddenly, I understood the allure of a shaved head, especially paired with a rakish goatee and a tiny hoop earring. He looked a bit like a pirate—and he also looked as if he liked Sophia, and her simple, curvy midnight-blue sheath, very much.

My whole family was under one roof, my parents, my siblings, their children, my daughter—and even my husband's son. I'd invited them back in August, with Nell's blessing, surprising Michael into speechlessness.

Well, momentary speechlessness, anyway. Michael was never without words for long.

"You don't have to do that, you know," he'd said. I'd told him that I'd called Sophia while we were grocery shopping on a Saturday afternoon, of all things, and he'd stopped dead beside the neatly arranged rows of spaghetti sauce and tomato paste. "It's Nell's wedding, and she might not want…"

I waved a box of linguine at him with airy confidence. "I already asked her, and she's fine with it. They're family, too, Michael. And it's something for Drew to look forward to, a reason for him to come and stay, see our home. Hell, he needs to meet Walter, if nothing else."

Michael laughed, but when we turned into the

frozen-foods section, he pushed me against the cold front of a door and kissed me until I blushed.

Even just six weeks ago, that Drew would even be able to come wasn't a sure thing. Turned out that bone marrow transplantation was as big a deal as transplanting any organ, and he was in the hospital for almost three weeks until the new cells engrafted properly. He was at risk for bleeding and all kinds of infection, which meant keeping him in isolation, and today he was only three months post-transplant, almost to the day. He was thin and still pale, and he'd lost a lot of his hair during the pretransplant chemo and radiation, but he was so alive, grateful, excited, interested, watching everything and everyone as if he'd be quizzed on it later.

"I told you he knows what he wants," Sophia said on the phone when she called to say they would drive down for the wedding. Her tone was rich with rueful pride. "He fought with the doctors, and then fought some more. But the truth is, he's doing better than anyone could have believed."

Emma, apparently, had believed it all along—and she'd taken an eventual visit from Drew as a given. She'd nattered at me to start cleaning up the guest room the day they'd discharged her from the hospital, and she hadn't let up until I handed her the reins of the project and told her to give it a shot. She'd taken a job at a summer day camp run by the YWCA, but most afternoons when she got home, she retreated upstairs with plastic storage bins, dust rags and paint samples. By the time Michael and I informed her that Drew and Sophia would be coming for Nell's wedding, she'd painted the room a soft spring green, made new curtains and throw pillows for the bed, and nudged me into buying a new comforter set that reminded me of sea glass, with stripes of clear green and blue and sand.

Not that she'd become all work and no play, of course. Whenever she wasn't working at the camp or working on the guest room, she was with Jesse—whenever he wasn't working at the supermarket. Their schedules didn't leave them a lot of time to be together, which I of course didn't mind, but by August I had to admit that they were really pretty devoted to each other. At least twice they'd spent the evening with Michael and me watching a DVD, which made me blink.

"See," Michael said on one of those occasions, as Emma followed Jesse out onto the dark front porch to say good-night. "Maybe all teenage couples aren't all hands and out-of-control hormones."

Of course, at that moment, the kids put their arms around each other to kiss good-night. I had to tug Michael away from the window when it was clear that neither Emma nor Jesse was afraid to use tongue.

Still, the summer had been a good one. Lucy and I had talked, finally, and spent a weekend together at the Maryland shore, drinking far too many margaritas and soaking up the sun. Michael had begun writing a new novel, and was constantly scribbling notes to himself on bits of napkins or the back of my grocery lists. And what had looked like a storm, especially where Emma was concerned, had blown through quickly. It had stripped away a bit of Emma's childhood, yes, but it had revealed a glimpse of the young woman she was becoming—a woman I would be proud to know.

A young woman who hadn't yet forgotten, I reminded myself as I watched her across the room, what childhood was for. She'd kicked off her shoes and was sliding across the floor with her grandfather in her stocking feet, her face flushed pink and her giggle a perfect echo of her five-year-old self.

I put my arm around Michael's waist and took a sip of my wine as the deejay queued up "Moondance." Nell and Jack had decided not to be formally announced—"Everyone just saw us say our vows ten minutes ago!" Nell had protested—but I knew this was their song. The crowd parted as Jack gathered Nell against him and she laid her head on his shoulder as they started to move.

"You might want to get a picture of this," Michael murmured in my ear, and I sputtered wine.

Crap. Being the maid of honor and the photographer at the same time wasn't easy, especially when my mind was so busy traveling back over the weeks needed to get here. Michael took my glass as I fetched my camera from a nearby table, and managed to get half a dozen perfect shots of the newlyweds dancing.

When I looked away from them, I found Drew holding out his hand to Emma, and I wriggled past other dancing couples to get a few shots of them, too.

I had dozens now—the photos I'd taken that day in the hospital waiting room, plus many more I'd shot in the weeks as we drove back and forth. There were more frames of Drew and Michael, too, and shots of Drew, Michael and Sophia—all kinds of permutations of the new family that we had become since May.

But they weren't the photos I planned to submit to Alicia for the gallery opening. I'd shot others over the summer, a series of the local families I'd thought about all those weeks ago, and another series of more whimsical shots—a collection of mismatched forks on a table at a flea market, laundry hanging on a line, pairs of shoes lined up beside a door.

The photos of us were too new, and too important, somehow. It wasn't that I didn't want anyone to know how our family had changed, more that I wanted to keep it safe and make a choice to respect all the people in it.

Love, I'd figured out, was never only about two people. I put my camera down and pulled Michael out to the dance floor, and put my arms around him just as the deejay put on a new song. The people around you were swept along in love's wake, and the bigger your love was, the more people it seemed to touch.

Michael and I had changed the world, just a little, by choosing to love each other. And that was a big responsibility, but it was also a gift— to ourselves and to the people we cared about. I'd learned that much, anyway.

And I knew, as Michael turned me on the floor with the candlelight flickering and the music a soft pulse in the background, his arms a familiar anchor around me, that it wasn't a gift I would ever take for granted again.

"What are you thinking about?" he murmured, his lips warm against my cheek.

"Nothing." I lifted my face to his and kissed him. "Everything. Love. Choices. Weddings. Pictures. I'd love to have a picture of us, just like this, to look at from time to time. Problem is, who would take it?"

He steered me out of the room and into the center hallway, then out onto the porch where the ceremony had been held. A few college kids in white shirts and black bow ties were stacking the chairs, but Michael ignored them as we swayed to the faint music.

"You don't need a picture of this," he said, and left a trail of light kisses along my cheekbone. "I'll dance with you anywhere you want, anytime."

"I'm counting on it," I whispered.

We couldn't quite hear the music anymore, and the porch was beginning to get chilly, but it didn't matter. We kept dancing.

* * * * *

*Celebrate 60 years of pure reading pleasure
with Harlequin® Books!*

*Harlequin Romance® is celebrating by
showering you with DIAMOND BRIDES in
February 2009.
Six stories that promise to bring a touch of
sparkle to your life, with diamond proposals
and dazzling weddings, sparkling brides and
gorgeous grooms!*

*Enjoy a sneak peek at Caroline Anderson's
TWO LITTLE MIRACLES,
available February 2009
from Harlequin Romance®.*

'I'VE FOUND HER.'

Max froze.

It was what he'd been waiting for since June, but now—now he was almost afraid to voice the question. His heart stalling, he leaned slowly back in his chair and scoured the investigator's face for clues. 'Where?' he asked, and his voice sounded rough and unused, like a rusty hinge.

'In Suffolk. She's living in a cottage.'

Living. His heart crashed back to life, and he sucked in a long, slow breath. All these months he'd feared—

'Is she well?'

'Yes, she's well.'

He had to force himself to ask the next question. 'Alone?'

The man paused. 'No. The cottage belongs to a man called John Blake. He's working away at the moment, but he comes and goes.'

God. He felt sick. So sick he hardly registered the next few words, but then gradually they sank in. 'She's got *what?*'

'Babies. Twin girls. They're eight months old.'

'Eight—?' he echoed under his breath. 'They must be his.'

He was thinking out loud, but the P.I. heard and corrected him.

'Apparently not. I gather they're hers. She's been there since mid-January last year, and they were born during the summer—June, the woman in the post office thought. She was more than helpful. I think there's been a certain amount of speculation about their relationship.'

He'd just bet there had. God, he was going to kill her. Or Blake. Maybe both of them.

'Of course, looking at the dates, she was presumably pregnant when she left you, so they could be yours, or she could have been having an affair with this Blake character before...'

He glared at the unfortunate P.I. 'Just stick to your job. I can do the math,' he snapped, swallowing the unpalatable possibility that she'd been unfaithful to him before she'd left. 'Where is she? I want the address.'

'It's all in here,' the man said, sliding a large envelope across the desk to him. 'With my invoice.'

'I'll get it seen to. Thank you.'

'If there's anything else you need, Mr Gallagher, any further information—'

'I'll be in touch.'

'The woman in the post office told me Blake was away at the moment, if that helps,' he added quietly, and opened the door.

Max stared down at the envelope, hardly daring to open it, but when the door clicked softly shut behind the P.I., he eased up the flap, tipped it and felt his breath jam in his throat as the photos spilled out over the desk.

Oh, lord, she looked gorgeous. Different, though. It took him a moment to recognise her, because she'd grown her hair, and it was tied back in a ponytail, making her look younger and somehow freer. The blond highlights were gone, and it was back to its natural soft golden-brown, with a little curl in the end of the ponytail that he wanted to thread his finger through and tug, just gently, to draw her back to him.

Crazy. She'd put on a little weight, but it suited her. She looked well and happy and beautiful, but oddly, considering how desperate he'd been for news of her for the past year—one year, three weeks and two days, to be exact— it wasn't only Julia who held his attention after the initial shock. It was the babies sitting side by side in a supermarket trolley. Two identical and absolutely beautiful little girls.

* * * * *

When Max Gallagher hires a P.I. to find his estranged wife, Julia, he discovers she's not alone—she has twin baby girls, and they might be his. Now workaholic Max has just two weeks to prove that he can be a wonderful husband and father to the family he wants to treasure.

Look for TWO LITTLE MIRACLES by
Caroline Anderson,
available February 2009
from Harlequin Romance®.

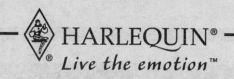

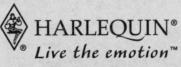

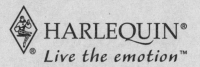

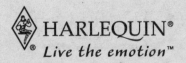

Harlequin® Historical
Historical Romantic Adventure!

*Imagine a time of chivalrous
knights and unconventional ladies,
roguish rakes and impetuous
heiresses, rugged cowboys
and spirited frontierswomen—
these rich and vivid tales will
capture your imagination!*

*Harlequin Historical . . .
they're too good to miss!*

HARLEQUIN®
Presents

The world's bestselling romance series...
The series that brings you your favorite authors,
month after month:

Helen Bianchin...Emma Darcy
Lynne Graham...Penny Jordan
Miranda Lee...Sandra Marton
Anne Mather...Carole Mortimer
Melanie Milburne...Michelle Reid

and many more talented authors!

Wealthy, powerful, gorgeous men...
Women who have feelings just like your own...
The stories you love, set in exotic, glamorous locations...

HARLEQUIN®
Presents

Seduction and Passion Guaranteed!

HPDIR08

www.eHarlequin.com

SPECIAL EDITION™

Emotional, compelling stories that capture the intensity of living, loving and creating a family in today's world.

Desire

Modern, passionate reads that are powerful and provocative.

nocturne

Dramatic and sensual tales of paranormal romance.

Romantic SUSPENSE

Romances that are sparked by danger and fueled by passion.